MEET THE FO

Fortune of the Mon

Age: 24

Vital Statistics: Long blond hair, chocolate-brown eyes and a comfortable bank account. The kind of girl who should have no trouble meeting a fella. And she doesn't. But meeting the *right* kind of fella, that's another story.

Claim to Fame: The youngest daughter of the Fortunado (Fortune) family. She's a daddy's girl, a wee bit impulsive and just a little high-maintenance. She always sees the glass as half-full.

Romantic Prospects: For reasons she cannot explain, she has always had bad luck when it comes to men. Could she have finally turned that corner?

"I still don't understand why Jake Brockton came up as a match for me on that dating app. I specifically requested an educated white-collar kind of guy, and Jake is a cowboy who dropped out of college.

"But maybe the app is smarter than I am. I've never met a guy like Jake before. He's as honest as the day is long. So maybe he's just a little gun-shy. My family is concerned that I'm falling too fast. As far as I'm concerned, though, I can't fall fast enough! My heart tells me he's The One. My head wonders why he's holding back..."

THE FORTUNES OF TEXAS:
The Lost Fortunes—Family secrets revealed!

Dear Reader,

Welcome back to Texas! And to my latest book for Harlequin Special Edition, *Her Secret Texas Valentine*. I'm delighted to once again have the opportunity to write a story for the Fortunes of Texas continuity.

When sweet (but slightly spoiled) Valene Fortunado hooks up to a dating app, she has no idea she is about to meet a man who isn't *anything* like what she imagined she wanted. Cowboy Jake Brockton doesn't tick any of her boxes. She was looking for a suit...and instead found a Stetson! But attraction is a funny thing. And so is love, as this seemingly mismatched pair quickly discover.

Jake has been badly burned in love in the past and has no real desire to get back into the saddle. But Valene is hard to resist...and with Valentine's Day just around the corner, he soon realizes they are a perfect match after all. Of course, the road to their happy ending is rocky, but true love always wins in the end.

I hope you enjoy Jake and Valene's story. I love hearing from readers and can be contacted at helenlaceyauthor@gmail.com or via my website or Facebook page to talk about horses, cowboys or how wonderful it is writing for Harlequin Special Edition. Happy reading!

Warmest wishes,

Helen Lacey

Her Secret Texas Valentine

Helen Lacey

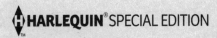
HARLEQUIN® SPECIAL EDITION

Special thanks and acknowledgment are given to Helen Lacey for her contribution to the Fortunes of Texas: The Lost Fortunes series.

Recycling programs
for this product may
not exist in your area.

ISBN-13: 978-1-335-57365-0

Her Secret Texas Valentine

Copyright © 2019 by Harlequin Books S.A.

HARLEQUIN®
www.Harlequin.com

Printed in U.S.A.

Helen Lacey grew up reading *Black Beauty* and *Little House on the Prairie*. These childhood classics inspired her to write her first book when she was seven, a story about a girl and her horse. She loves writing for Harlequin Special Edition, where she can create strong heroes with soft hearts and heroines with gumption who get their happily-ever-afters. For more about Helen, visit her website, helenlacey.com.

Books by Helen Lacey

Harlequin Special Edition

The Cedar River Cowboys

Three Reasons to Wed
Lucy & the Lieutenant
The Cowgirl's Forever Family
Married to the Mom-to-Be
The Rancher's Unexpected Family
A Kiss, a Dance & a Diamond
The Secret Son's Homecoming

The Fortunes of Texas

A Fortunes of Texas Christmas

The Prestons of Crystal Point

The CEO's Baby Surprise

Claiming His Brother's Baby

Harlequin Serialization

Secrets of the A-List, Part 5

Visit the Author Profile page
at Harlequin.com for more titles.

For my parents,
who always encouraged me to read, to write and
to dream. I miss you both more than words can say.

Chapter One

Twenty-four-year-old real estate agent Valene Fortunado had no illusions about her love life.

She didn't have one.

One lousy date after another over the past six months had made that abundantly clear.

It wasn't like she needed a man to *complete* her. After all, she wasn't the kind of woman to get caught up in grand gestures or romantic nonsense. Okay...maybe she *was*. Maybe she only acted as though she was a career woman, first and foremost.

Still...a *good* date every now and then would fill some of her lonelier nights.

And not that she was really lonely, either. It was just that since both her sisters and two of her brothers had found love, they kept insisting that her white knight was around the corner. Valene wasn't so sure. Maybe her white knight had galloped past on his way through her neck of the woods and failed to notice she was standing there. Maybe she had been too wrapped up in her latest open house or contract negotiation to spot him riding by. She *had* been known to have blinders on when it came to the opposite sex.

Which was why she decided to log into My Perfect Match and let an app find her a date.

How bad could it be?

That was the question she *should* have asked herself two disastrous dates ago.

Date number one was so dull he could have been a cardboard cutout. And he spent the whole two and a half excruciating hours talking about himself, his license plate collection and his beloved mother. Date number two barely said a word and was so scruffy he looked like he'd been wearing the same clothes for a week. Not that Valene was hung up on appearances…but at the very least she expected her date to wear a clean shirt and take off his baseball cap during dinner. Novice mistake— first dates should be over coffee, not dinner. There was no easy escape during a three-course sit-down meal that might include a bottle of wine and several hours of conversation. Next time, she would meet someone over coffee and make sure she had a quick exit strategy in case it turned into a disaster.

Because there would be a next time.

Valene wasn't about to give up simply because she'd made a few rookie errors.

She was mostly well behaved and did the right thing. Her parents adored her, and she wanted to make them proud. Plus, she'd always endeavored to be a proactive kind of girl and had never been accused of lacking gumption or courage. But she was determined to be more prudent in her choices. If both her sisters, Schuyler and Maddie, could find love with the men of their dreams, Valene expected nothing less for herself. As long as he ticked all the right boxes.

Looks…well, she wasn't too fussy, but nice eyes and broad shoulders would be a bonus.

Money…enough that he didn't expect her to pay for every meal and had a nice car.

Smarts…a college education and a good job were a must.

How hard could it be? Her sisters had managed it— so could she. Not that she was going to let the whole idea take up too much time or attention. She had more important things on her mind.

It had been a busy few months with way too much drama for her liking. And too much family. Hers and everyone else's. Fortunados. Robinsons. Fortunes. Mendozas. Family life wasn't simple anymore. She had relatives coming out of the woodwork. And things to do.

Like saving the family business.

Too many things had gone pear-shaped at Fortunado Real Estate in the past couple of months. Too many deals had been lost for it to be simple coincidence. And she loathed thinking it was merely bad judgment on their part. Sure, they'd lost sales and contracts to other real estate agents before, but this felt different. It felt… *personal*. As though someone was specifically targeting her family's business. And Valene wouldn't sit by and allow that to happen—not on her watch.

Still, she needed to make time for herself. Which was why she was on her way to meet date number three.

As she headed for the Houston coffee place, she caught a glimpse of herself in a flower shop window, pleased that she'd worn a dress and heels that flattered her curves and made her look taller than her five foot three. She glanced at her expression. Not too eager. Not too resistant, either. Just ready for whatever happened. And she was ready. She had her sister's number on speed dial in her cell phone and knew every exit in the coffee place to escape in two seconds if need be.

Valene took a deep breath that added some resolve to her suddenly dwindling courage.

Third time lucky, she told herself.

She remained in the doorway and looked around. Blue shirt, she reminded herself. Look for a man wearing a blue shirt. That was the text message she'd received. She spotted three potentials. The first was a guy at the counter paying for two tall frappés. Right age. Tallish. Dark hair. Then she heard him haggling with the barista about a tip before he grabbed the drinks and walked directly past her without her being so much as a blip on his radar. *Not him, thank God.* Valene took another deep breath. She looked toward the second blue-shirted candidate. Not as tall, and thicker set. But he had a nice face and actually looked up and smiled at her. *Okay...he looks normal enough.* She was about to smile back when another woman passed her and headed for his table. The pair kissed briefly and then the woman sat down. Right. Not him, either.

She glanced toward the booth seat and saw candidate number three had his back to her. Broad shoulders and short blond hair, and a nice blue shirt. He looked so good from the back, she hoped it was him. From his online profile, she knew her date's name was Jake and that he worked outside the city. The few texts they'd exchanged had been articulate and humorous enough to pique her interest and make her want to meet him.

Nothing ventured...nothing gained.

She'd always had gumption, according to her family. Now was the time to show some. And if it didn't work out, so be it.

Valene pushed back her shoulders and walked through the coffeehouse.

Dating apps.

Jake Brockton figured that signing on to one was up there as one of the stupidest things he'd ever done. But he'd promised his sister he'd try it, and he was a man of his word. And it was just coffee. Not a date. Nothing that required too much time or attention. And he could bail as soon as felt the interaction going south.

He glanced at his watch. She was late. He hated that.

Jake had no tolerance for tardiness. He hadn't gotten to where he was by being lazy or disorganized. It had been through grit and a steely determination to be the best version of himself he could possibly be.

Too bad his ex-wife hadn't thought so.

He pushed the memory from his mind and tapped his fingers on the table. He really didn't have time to waste on romantic entanglements. The ranch kept him busy 24/7 and he wasn't about to get seriously involved with anyone. Still, he'd promised Cassidy, and he always kept his promises to his baby sister.

Conscious that someone was standing by the booth seat, Jake turned his head and quickly sucked in a sharp breath.

A woman stood barely two feet away. She was petite but surprisingly curvy, with long blond hair and brown eyes the color of Belgian chocolate. His gut recognized an instant reaction, and he swallowed hard, taking in her perfectly aligned features and lovely curves. She smiled, and her mouth curled at the corners.

His date.

They'd shared a few text messages the day before. Nothing too personal. Just their first names, interests and a time and place to meet. She'd seemed friendly and had added humorous emojis to her texts.

He got to his feet in a microsecond and held out his hand.

"Hi," he said quietly. "I'm Jake Brockton."

She stepped a little closer and took his hand, and he experienced an inexplicable tightening in his chest as their skin connected. Her eyes widened fractionally, as though she was experiencing the same reaction and then she quickly withdrew her hand.

"Valene Fortunado," she said, her voice huskier than he'd expected. "But everyone calls me Val."

Fortunado? He'd heard the name but wasn't sure where. Jake nodded and signaled to the waitress. "Coffee?"

"That would be nice," she said as she placed her small bag on the seat. "I've been here before. You?"

Jake shook his head. "But my sister told me the coffee is good."

As small talk went, it was pretty benign, and he ignored the way his insides twitched. She was very attractive…more than he'd expected. More than he wanted. In his experience, beautiful women were nothing but trouble and potential heartache.

The waitress arrived and he listened, amused, as his date ordered a single-shot, low-fat, vanilla soy latte with extra cinnamon. He asked for a tall black and waited until the waitress disappeared before he spoke again.

"You're very pretty."

She raised one brow, clearly not expecting the compliment. "Thank you. You're not so bad yourself."

Jake laughed softly. "Can I ask you something?"

She nodded. "Sure."

"Why are you using a dating app?"

"Why are you?" she shot back, smiling.

"My sister made me do it," he admitted. "She thinks I spend too much time alone."

Her lovely brow arched higher. "And do you?"

"Probably. Occupational habit."

"What do you do?" she asked.

Jake expelled an even breath. "I work on a ranch."

She sat back in her seat, her head tilted at a gentle angle. "Doing what?"

"Ranching stuff."

She smiled slightly. "I'm a city girl, so I'll need a little more information."

"Ranching," he replied. "Mustering cattle. Horse breaking."

Her brows came together. "Like…a cowboy?"

He nodded. "Exactly."

"I've never been on a date with a cowboy before."

"Really?" He grinned. "Then you've led a sheltered life. This is Texas—cowboy capital of the nation."

She laughed, and the sound reverberated in his chest. "I know that, too. I was born and raised in Houston. What about you?"

"I was raised in San Antonio until I was twelve, but I was born in Stafford, just outside Houston," he said.

"That's a nice spot. I sold a dude ranch there once," she said idly. "Property values hold steady."

Jake rested his elbows on the table. "You owned a dude ranch?"

She shook her head and grinned, waiting while the waitress approached with their order before speaking again. "No, it's what I do for a living."

"Selling dude ranches?"

"Selling real estate," she corrected. "I work in my family's business."

He recalled seeing that she was self-employed on her profile. And now he knew why her surname seemed familiar. He knew of Fortunado Real Estate. They were one of the biggest in the city, and her family was connected to the famous Fortunes of Texas. "Do you enjoy it?"

"Mostly," she replied. "I split my time between both the Austin and Houston offices and like any business, it has its ups and downs. It's a little more down than up at the moment, but I always look on the bright side."

Jake stirred a little sugar into his coffee. "I'm glad to hear it. So, you didn't answer my question."

"Which one?"

He met her gaze. "Why the dating app?"

She shrugged fractionally. "It's simply a way to meet people."

"People?"

Her cheeks spotted with color. "Guys. Or *a* guy. You know, Mr. Wonderful and all that." She spooned the froth off her beverage. "But the truth is, if you'd turned out to be a cardboard cutout or one of the great unwashed, I was going to make this my third and last attempt."

Jake laughed softly. "You've done this before?"

She held up two fingers. "And both disastrous."

"I take it one was dull and the other had an issue with personal hygiene?"

She chuckled and he noticed that her brown eyes had flecks of gold in them. Damn, she really was pretty.

"Exactly," she said on a sigh.

"And how am I comparing so far?"

Her eyes widened, and she bit her lower lip for a moment. "Well, from here you look very much like flesh and blood. And you smell nice."

He laughed again and realized he'd done quite a lot of that since she'd arrived. "So, Valene, tell me about yourself."

She didn't break their gaze. "I'm twenty-four. Single, obviously. I work for my family's real estate business. My parents are wonderful and still happily in love after thirtysomething years of marriage. I'm the youngest of six children and am considered to be somewhat spoiled. I have my own condo in the city and a fiercely protective bulldog. I'm allergic to passion fruit and I love chocolate. You?"

Jake drank some coffee and looked at her. "I'm thirty-two. Single, obviously," he said, echoing her words. "I work on a ranch near Fulshear, outside Houston. My father died over a decade ago, and my mom still grieves him every day. I have a younger sister named Cassidy who is considered somewhat spoiled. I have a very *unprotective* collie mix called Sheba who tries to sleep on the end of my bed every night. I'm not allergic to anything I know of and I can take or leave chocolate."

It was a vague introduction, since he wasn't about to start saying too much about himself to a stranger. But she seemed nice enough, and what harm could a little flirtation do?

"It's nice to meet you, Jake," she said, still smiling.

"Likewise, Valene."

"Do you like being a cowboy?" she asked.

"It has its up and downs," he said, mimicking her earlier words as he smiled. "It's physically hard work, but rewarding. It's all I've done since I left college."

"Where did you graduate?" She sipped her latte and

looked at him over the rim of her mug. "The University of Houston?"

"No."

"Rice University?"

"I dropped out before the second semester."

Jake waited for her expression to change, for disappointment or censure to show on her pretty face. But to her credit, she didn't appear fazed by what he'd described as his meager education. Or his occupation.

"Oh, I see," she said and continued to sip her coffee. "And you said you've been working on the ranch ever since?"

Jake nodded. "We moved from San Antonio to the ranch when I was twelve. My father worked there for a long time."

"And when he died you took over his job?" she asked.

Jake shrugged. "Someone had to fill his boots. So, Valene, why are you single?" he asked, abruptly changing the subject.

"I'm high maintenance," she said and grinned. "Scared?"

"Not at all," he replied, watching the way her mouth curled at the edges and thinking how sexy it was. It had been a long time since he'd been attracted to someone. But she was funny and flirtatious, and he was discovering that he enjoyed her company. "But I'm not sure I believe you."

She shrugged. "I work long hours, and that doesn't leave me a lot of time for socializing. But lately…"

Her words trailed off and he raised both brows questioningly. "Lately?"

"Both my sisters and one of my brothers have recently gotten married, and another brother got engaged," she explained and sighed. "I feel left out, I guess, as if romance and love have passed me by."

"And is that what you want?" he queried. "Romance and love?"

She shrugged again. "Doesn't everyone?" She turned back and then made a face. "To be honest, I'd settle for someone to share a pizza, watch a movie and snuggle with."

Jake smiled, trying to recall the last time he'd snuggled with anyone. His ex-wife, Patrice, hadn't exactly been the *snuggling* type. But Valene Fortunado, with her lovely hair, soft brown eyes and subtle curves, made him think that it was time he got back to really living and reconnecting with the world.

"What kind of movies do you like?" he asked and finished his coffee.

She chuckled. "Ah…actually, I like a little zombie action."

Jake laughed. "No chick flicks?"

She shook her head. "Not really. Just zombies and fright-night kinds of films."

Jake winced. "Then I guess we're not going to do that pizza and a movie thing," he said, smiling as he shrugged. "Pity."

Her lips curled. "You don't like scary movies?"

"I don't like clowns," he admitted. "And one always seems to turn up in that kind of movie."

She laughed again, so softly, so delightfully, that Jake's belly rolled over.

"You're scared of clowns?"

"Not scared," he corrected quickly. "I just don't like them all that much."

"Tough guy like you," she shot back, still chuckling. "In the movies, cowboys aren't afraid of anything."

"I'm not afraid," he reiterated, enjoying her teasing. "Just…cautious. It's those big feet and red noses… they're kinda freaky."

She laughed again. "Well, if we ever go on a date to a carnival or circus, I promise to protect you from the clowns terrorizing the midway."

Jake stared at her, relaxed back in the booth seat and spoke. "Would you like to?"

Her head tilted fractionally. "Would I like to what?"

"Go on a date?"

Valene's heart was beating like a jackhammer. Jake Brockton was utterly gorgeous. His eyes were clear blue, his face perfectly angled and proportioned, his blond hair the kind that begged for fingers to thread through it. And the rest of him was to-die-for hot. His shoulders were broad, his arms well muscled, and she was certain the rest of him would hold up to her and every other woman on the planet's scrutiny. She couldn't recall ever seeing a man fill out a chambray shirt the way he did. And he had nice hands—strong looking, with long blunt fingers, neat nails and a few calluses that signified hard work. Yes, Jake Brockton was about as masculine and attractive a man as she'd ever met.

Plus, he seemed to like her.

Unfortunately, the good-looking cowboy didn't tick any of her boxes.

No career. No college education. And probably no money. She couldn't be certain, but surely ranch hands weren't paid extravagant salaries. She was disappointed through to her core.

But what harm could a single date do?

It wasn't a marriage proposal. Or a lifelong commitment. And she didn't have anyone else knocking on her door asking for her time and attention. She thought about it, looking at his handsome face again. And decided she'd live a little.

"Sure," she said as casually as she could manage. "Why not."

"Friday night?"

She nodded. "Where?"

He named a small Italian restaurant a few streets away. "Shall I pick you up?"

"I'll meet you there," she replied. "Um…that's a popular place. I'm not sure we could get a reservation this late. Perhaps somewhere else would be easier."

He looked amused by her caution. "I'll text you a time once I make a reservation."

She wasn't convinced he'd get a table, but she agreed. "Ah…great."

"Would you like more coffee?"

She smiled a little. The man certainly wasn't short on manners, and she realized he was an intriguing mix of rough and smooth. There was no denying his earthy roots. His clothes were clean and tidy, but the closer she looked, the more she noticed how the shirt was frayed a little around the cuffs, and how the Stetson sitting on the seat beside him was clearly well used. And despite the air of civility oozing from him, there was nothing urban about Jake Brockton. He was country through and through. Not what she wanted. Not anything like what she wanted. Except…his blue eyes were unbelievably mesmerizing. And his clean-shaven jaw made her fingertips itch with the urge to trace a pattern along his cheek and chin.

Awareness and attraction mingled through her blood and she managed a tight smile, conscious that he was watching her intently. She tried to recall the last time she'd been as interested in a man, and the lingering memory of her first real boyfriend flittered along the edges of her mind. But Diego hadn't hung around. And it turned out he was only ambitious and interested in her family's money and connections rather than her. He wanted a career in real estate and thought she was his meal ticket, and he showed little shame in making it clear he deserved it after putting up with being her boyfriend for a year. After that, a little older and wiser, she'd dated Hugh. He was handsome and polite and from a nice family—his father was a friend of her father's, and they'd been set up with the expectation that they would be perfect for one another. Yes, Hugh was perfect—he had perfect looks and manners and a career in the finance sector, and for five months she'd been convinced they would have a predictable happily-ever-after. But there was very little spark between them. Actually, no spark. Zilch. So it was an easy decision to end things between them. He was disappointed. She was wife material, he said. She shouldn't have high expectations. After that, she'd begun to believe that maybe the spark thing was a myth. But then, over the course of the past year, both her sisters and two of her brothers had fallen madly in love and it got Val thinking that maybe that big love really did exist.

"Why are *you* single, Jake?" she asked bluntly.

"I've been too busy," he said vaguely.

She gave him a disbelieving look. "Really?"

"That's the truth, but I guess I'm still looking for my perfect match."

She chuckled. "Do you think there's such a thing?"

He shrugged lightly. "I'd like to think so. I'm not so sure anymore."

"Do you want kids?"

His expression altered for a nanosecond, as though he was lost in thought. Finally, he spoke again. "Yes, one day. You?"

"I'm pretty sure I want kids…one day."

"You're only twenty-four," he reminded her. "You have plenty of time to think about kids."

Her belly did an odd kind of dive. "I know. But I think it's more about being with the right person, rather than being the right age."

He nodded. "I think you're right. So, tell me about your two disastrous dates."

She laughed lightly. "Oh, my God, they were unbelievably bad. The first guy collected license plates from every state and talked nonstop about his mother. And the second one—he wore a baseball cap backward. But," she said and flashed him a smile, "third time's the charm."

He met her gaze. "I'm really glad your first two dates were duds."

Valene kept the visual contact. "Me too. Anyhow, I should probably get going. I have an open house at noon and need to get back to the office beforehand. But it was nice to meet you."

"You too," he said and waited for her to stand before he got to his feet.

He excused himself for a moment and headed for the counter to pay the check before Valene had a chance to offer to pay her share. When he returned to her, she was halfway to the entrance. He opened the door and let her pass, and they stepped out into the sunlight.

"My car's right here," she said and used the beeper to unlock her silver Lexus, which was parked directly outside the coffeehouse. "Yours?"

He jerked a thumb in the direction of a beaten-up blue Ranger parked on the other side of the road. There was faded writing on the side of the truck that she couldn't make out. Okay…so he had a crappy car. The fact that he was utterly gorgeous made up for that shortcoming. Valene tried to drag her gaze away but couldn't help looking him up and down. It should be illegal, she thought to herself as her skin prickled all over, for a man to look that good in chambray and denim.

"Well, thanks for meeting me, Jake," she said easily and held out her hand. "I had a nice time."

He took her hand, and electricity shot up her arm. "Likewise, Valene. I'll see you Friday."

For a moment, she could have sworn he swayed a little closer. Of course, he wouldn't try to kiss her. That would be outrageous, presumptuous and completely out of line. But still, her lips tingled foolishly and she let out a long and disappointed sigh.

Don't get ahead of yourself, Val. It was just coffee and conversation.

He released her hand and she quickly got into her car. When she pulled away from the curb and caught a glimpse of him in the rearview mirror, her thought surprised her. She'd suddenly developed a thing for cowboys.

Chapter Two

"So," Schuyler asked over brunch the following day. "How did it go?"

They were eating at the office, chowing down on gourmet chicken salads and freshly squeezed juice that their other sister, Maddie, had supplied. Her oldest sister commuted between Austin and Houston most weeks, and Schuyler had driven in from Austin the day before and was staying for a couple of days. They had ditched the break room and were seated around the big oak table in the boardroom.

"It was nice," Valene replied and sipped on a guava and pineapple drink. "Like I said."

"But he's a penniless cowboy?" Maddie asked bluntly.

Val shrugged. "I didn't ask to see his bank statements. He was nice, very charming and funny."

Maddie, always the most serious of the trio, looked

skeptical. "I can't believe you got matched up with a ranch hand. Didn't you say you specifically wanted an educated, white-collar kind of guy?"

She shrugged again. "I don't know. Perhaps he fudged the questionnaire."

"It's possible," Schuyler said and frowned.

"What a jerk," Maddie added.

But the more Val thought about it, the less likely Maddie's opinion seemed. There was something refreshingly candid and honest about Jake. Of course, it could be that she was still gaga over his broad shoulders and blue eyes and didn't want to see the truth right in front of her. But she was convinced that he was exactly as he appeared—a workingman, honest and down to earth. And as hot as Hades.

"We could google him," Schuyler suggested.

Val waved a hand. "Absolutely not. I'm not going to go stalker and start checking out social media profiles and that sort of thing. I want to be a grown-up about this. And I know this might sound silly, but I don't want to jinx it, okay?"

"What do you mean?" Schuyler asked.

"It means," Val said, a little impatiently, "that he was nice, and we had a good time over coffee, like I said. And we're going out for dinner tomorrow night."

"Do you think that's a good idea?" Maddie asked soberly. "I mean, if he's not the kind of guy you think you could get serious about, why bother getting to know him?"

Schuyler laughed. "You're such a snob, Maddie."

"I'm a realist," her sister defended. "And you've said it yourself, you want a man who ticks certain boxes. Sounds like he only ticks the 'looks good in a pair of jeans' box."

Both her sisters laughed, but Val wasn't amused. They were making fun, and for some reason, that bothered her. "We'll just see what happens."

"Well," Schuyler said dramatically, "I think it's great that you're getting out. And if this one doesn't work out, you can try again. But maybe redefine your criteria a little."

Maddie had a serious look on her face. "I'm not trying to be a party pooper, but you need to tread carefully and slowly when it comes to romance."

"Like you did?" Val shot back, brows up. "Weren't you the one who took you and Zach out of the colleague and friend zone when you planted that kiss on him at the Thirsty Ox? How long did it take you to jump into Zach's bed after that?"

Schuyler started wagging a few fingers and counting before Maddie shushed them both. "Okay…don't take *my* lead. All I'm saying is, don't be hasty. If he's right for you, then he'll wait. You're my baby sister and I'll always worry about you."

"I know," Val obliged. "And I appreciate your concern. But believe me, I'm not about to rush into anything. I know how everyone thinks I'm impulsive, but in this instance, I'm going to take my time and get to know someone before I make any big moves. Besides, I'm too busy with work to spend too much time on romance. If I don't start closing more deals," she said and glanced toward Maddie, who along with her überhandsome husband, Zach McCarter, had become joint CEO of Fortunado Real Estate since their father had retired, "Dad's going to insist you fire me."

"Ha," Schuyler said with mock horror. "No chance. You're Daddy's girl. He'll never allow Maddie or Zach to fire you. You are the golden girl and his number two protégée."

Val laughed, because they all knew Maddie had been their father's number one protégée.

"That's true," Val said and grinned. "I am Dad's favorite."

Maddie tossed a piece of lettuce in her direction. "And modest. Speaking of which, do our parents know you're on the hunt for a man?" Maddie asked.

Val rolled her eyes. "I'd hardly call it a hunt. I met Jake for coffee, not a commitment ceremony. And Dad and Mom generally stay out of my love life."

"Except for Hugh," Schuyler reminded her. "He was handpicked."

"Dad worries about gold diggers," Maddie said on a sigh. "And since you're so easily influenced and like to party, they probably thought they were doing the right thing."

"Gosh, I have a terrible reputation," she said tartly, trying to remember the last time she actually *did* go to a party. "Young and impulsive and likely to get into all kinds of trouble. Oh, hang on," she said and smiled. "That was you, Schuyler, getting cozy with the Mendozas so you could wrangle an introduction to our newly discovered Fortune relatives. And then falling in love with one of the sexy Mendoza men."

Of course, every word was true. Schuyler had integrated herself into the Mendoza family, specifically by getting a job working at the Mendoza Winery, and then by falling in love with Carlo Mendoza. It was a series of events, jump-started by discovering that the Fortunados were related to the infamous Fortune family. The very idea that they were connected to the Fortunes had sent a curious Schuyler on a mission to find out the whole truth. They discovered that their grandfather was actually Julius Fortune, and that their dad, Kenneth Fortunado, was one of his many illegitimate children dotted around the state and even the country. Their grandmother had signed a confidentiality agreement with Julius, but also being something of a free spirit, had changed Kenneth's name to Fortunado as a way of not completely complying to Julius's demands. Learning that, Schuyler had been determined to get acquainted with the Fortune branch of the family. That's how she ended up at the Mendoza Winery, pretending to be a waitress. The Mendozas and the Fortunes were interlaced by marriage. Turned out Julius's son Jerome Fortune, who was known as tech billionaire Gerald Robinson—their uncle—had a daughter who was married to one of the Mendoza cousins. The link was enough to get Schuyler's crazy mind into thinking she could somehow bring the families together.

Valene hadn't taken much interest at the time, since she'd been neck-deep in work and wanted to prove she could be as ambitious and successful at Fortunado Real Estate as her sister Maddie. But now the truth was out. They were really Fortunes—as their free-spirited grandmother had enjoyed an affair with the philandering Julius. Valene had learned to accept the fact that she had an incredibly complicated family tree. It wasn't unusual to see an article on the internet or in the paper about the family. In fact, it wasn't that long ago that a journalist named Ariana Lamonte had done an exposé on *all* of Gerald Robinson's children, including the ones he'd sired out of wedlock. Yeah, complicated didn't really cover it. Particularly now that Gerald Robinson, aka Jerome Fortune, had left his embittered wife, Charlotte, and had sought refuge in the arms of the first and only love of his life, Deborah—who had borne him three illegitimate sons decades earlier.

Yes, the Fortunado/Fortune/Mendoza connection was about as complicated as it got.

"Okay," Schuyler said and grinned. "I'll admit that I'm the flake in the family."

"What does that make me?" Maddie queried.

"The workaholic," Val said lightly. "And I'm the spoiled brat. I know, since our brothers have told me that repeatedly over the years."

"You're not spoiled," Schuyler defended. "But you're the youngest, and since we've already established that you're Daddy's favorite, you know you have to get labeled as something. But now I think we should check out this Jake on social media and see what he's hiding."

Val rolled her eyes. "He's not hiding anything."

"Everyone is hiding something," Maddie said, her mouth flattened. "What's his last name?"

"I'm not saying," Val replied, standing her ground. "I'm not going to do anything other than go on a nice and respectable date with the man."

Schuyler made a dramatic sound. "Oh, I see, you actually *like* him."

Val waved an impatient hand. She loved her sisters… but sometimes they were impossibly bossy and interfering. "We spent an hour together. I'd hardly call that enough time to form any kind of opinion."

"I'm not so sure about that," Maddie said seriously. "I was pining for Zach for years after the first time I laid eyes on him."

"But underneath your corporate and workaholic demeanor, you're a soppy sentimentalist," Val said and chuckled. "And I'm a realist."

They all laughed, and it was so nice to spend some

quality time with her sisters. Since both of them had married, and Schuyler had moved to Austin to be with Carlo, she'd missed their company. Of course, she still regularly saw Maddie at both the Houston and Austin offices, but that was work. She had friends, but other than her bestie, Adele, no one came close to the affection she felt for her siblings. She even missed hanging out with her brothers. Particularly Connor, who lived in Denver and was always a great source of advice and counsel.

Growing up as the youngest Fortunado child had had its difficult moments. For one, her parents were overprotective of her and often treated her as though she were eighteen and not twenty-four. Since her father had retired and he and her mother had begun traveling, their stranglehold had lessened a little, but she still spoke to both her parents every few days. Case in point: she hadn't told her parents she was using My Perfect Match to find a man, otherwise she knew her father would start handing out her number to people he thought were suitable for his youngest, beloved child.

She packed up what was left of her lunch and gave each of her sisters a hug. "I have to get back to work. I'm showing an estate in Bunker Hill this afternoon."

"The McGovern place?" Maddie inquired, quickly in CEO mode.

"That's the one," she said and shrugged. "I have a buyer from Arizona, a couple who are transferring to Houston for work. We video chatted last time I did an open house, and they seem interested in the property."

"But?" Maddie asked, always picking up on Val's body language.

"They're going in at under three fifty per square foot."

"Median price is what?" Maddie queried. "About four hundred?"

She nodded. "Yeah…so we'll see. The husband really likes the place, but his wife is a banker and is naturally going to try to screw the owners with a lower offer."

Maddie's brows rose quickly. "Please tell me you're not using that terminology with the clients?"

Val laughed. She loved Maddie, but sometimes her oldest sister was too uptight. "Of course not," she assured her boss and smoothed a hand over her perfectly tight chignon. "I am always at my professional best when I'm with a client."

"Well, as long as you let your hair down with your hot cowboy on Friday night," Schuyler said and chuckled.

Your hot cowboy…

Her skin turned uncharacteristically warm at the thought of Jake Brockton.

"Would you stop encouraging her to be as reckless as you?" Maddie scolded her sister.

Val was still smiling as she left the boardroom and headed up the hall. She passed her brother-in-law Zach McCarter and hiked a thumb in the direction of the boardroom. He nodded and grinned, clearly amused that she knew he would be looking for the wife he obviously adored. Val liked Zach; he was a good boss and a great businessman. She'd learned a lot from him since he'd moved to Houston from the San Antonio office. The transition had been at her father's behest, of course, before her dad had retired. Kenneth had pitted Maddie and Zach against one another in a contest to secure the top job once he retired, and over the course of the rivalry, they had fallen crazily in love.

She was still smiling as she entered her office and

was moving around her desk when her cell phone beeped. She checked the text message instantly.

It was her hot cowboy.

Toscano's. Seven o'clock. Looking forward to it. Jake.

She grinned when she noticed the smiling emoji, wondering how he'd wrangled a reservation at one of the most popular restaurants in Houston. She texted back quickly and tucked the cell into her pocket.

She had a date.

And for the first time in a long time, Val didn't feel quite so alone.

"Seriously, could you be any more evasive?"

Jake made an impatient sound at the whiny voice rattling in his ear. The same voice that had been demanding answers to a barrage of personal questions for the last five minutes.

"Cass," he said quietly, "I told you, it's none of your business."

"But it was my idea," she wailed and came around his left side, ignoring the fact he was hitching up the cinch on his horse and she was very much in the way. "I suggested the dating app to begin with."

The big gelding sidestepped and stomped its foot. Jake loved his baby sister, but sometimes she was as annoying as a buzzing mosquito. And about as relentless. She'd been at him the moment she got home from college for the weekend, demanding to know how his coffee dates went. Well, date, in the singular, because he'd canceled the two other dates he'd made once he'd met the vivacious and beautiful Valene Fortunado. He'd never been a player, and dating more than one woman didn't sit right.

"Cassidy," he said, calling his sister by her full name, "button up, will you. I've got work to do."

She huffed and swished her flaming-red ponytail. "Sometimes you are such a killjoy, Jake. If you hadn't taken my advice, you never would have met this goddess."

He turned his head and frowned. "And not once did I use that word," he reminded her. "Remember that when you start telling Mom how you're playing cupid."

His sister laughed. "You said she was pretty."

"She was. She is. But I don't want to make more of it than it was. Coffee and conversation," he said, his voice sterner. "That's it."

"But you're seeing her tonight, right?"

He nodded slowly. "Right."

"You should take flowers," Cassidy suggested. "Women love flowers. And wear a suit. And don't take that crappy old truck of yours. Make sure you drive the Sierra. I don't know why you bought the thing— you never take it out of the garage. You'd rather drive around in that old Ranger that you've had since you were sixteen."

Jake wasn't about to argue, since Cassidy had a point. He did prefer the Ranger. But he often had business dealings that required more class than the beat-up Ford that his father had taught him to drive in so many years ago. Sentiment made him hang on to the old truck. And memory. And the acknowledgment of where he had come from, where his roots were, and how far he'd come since his dad had been the foreman of the Double Rock Ranch.

Jake had been raised on the ranch since he was

twelve and Cassidy a newborn. Along with their mother, they'd lived in the cottage behind the main house, and their life had been happy and fulfilling. Jake loved the land and the work, but he'd also gotten good grades in high school, so college was the obvious next step. But when his father had died suddenly from a heart attack when he was eighteen, he'd quickly hightailed it back home from school and stepped into his father's boots. If he hadn't, his mom and sister would have been forced to leave the ranch, and that was unthinkable.

But he understood why Cassidy made the comment about the suit and the truck. Jake had no illusions. Valene was city while he was country. But he wasn't an uneducated hick, even though she might think he was. True, she hadn't made any condescending remarks when he'd admitted to dropping out of college, but he sensed some level of disappointment. He did admire the way she'd kept that feeling to herself, though. And he liked how she had asked him about his work and hadn't made any negative remarks about his occupation. He knew from experience that some women measured a man's worth by the weight of his wallet.

Like Patrice...

He'd pined for her through high school, but she was with the it crowd, and Jake was definitely not on her radar. Years later, that changed. Patrice did notice him. And because he was still stuck on her, Jake didn't hesitate in falling head over heels in love with her, not realizing she was cold and calculating and not to be trusted. He learned his life lessons the hard way. Through Patrice's betrayal and humiliation, his heart hardened, and he was determined he'd never be made a fool of again.

Jake gently grabbed Cassidy's shoulders and ushered her out of the way. He checked the cinch, grabbed the reins and effortlessly sprang into the saddle. "Try to stay out of trouble, will you. I'll be back in an hour or so."

"We haven't finished this conversation," she reminded him, hands on hips.

Jake shook his head. "See ya, kid. Don't forget to study while you're here this weekend."

Cassidy was in her third year at college, but she was easily distracted. He loved her, though, and would walk through fire for her and his mom. He reined the gelding and headed from the corral, meeting up with two of the ranch hands who'd been waiting patiently by the stables.

"Sorry, boys," he said, though no apology was necessary. They all knew how irritating and adorable Cassidy could be.

"No worries, boss," the older of the duo replied. Kris had been on the Double Rock Ranch longer than he had. Jake still winced every time one of the ranch hands called him boss, but he'd worked hard to get where he was, and everyone on the Double Rock knew it and respected him for it. "I got a younger sister myself. Nothin' but trouble."

They all laughed as they headed off. When they passed the main house, Jake slowed down a fraction. The renovations were finally being finished, something that was a long time coming. For years the previous owners had let the home fall into disrepair, but things on the Double Rock were slowly changing. The ranch, situated in Fort Bend County, was a forty-minute drive to Houston and just under four hundred acres. Prime land, dotted with oak and pecan trees, it was predominantly cattle and horses and operated a highly lucrative Wagyu beef business. Jake loved the Double Rock and couldn't imagine living anywhere else.

He spent the following hour checking the perimeter

fences on the west side of the property, ending up down by the creek. From there he had a great view of the rear of the house and the back deck that was currently being redone. Several contractors were working on the place, and he waved to a couple when they spotted him.

By the time he was finished with the fences, it was past four o'clock. He headed for the office in the stables and did paperwork for an hour and then made his way to the bunkhouse to shower and change. Since Cassidy was staying for the weekend, he'd planned on bunking with the ranch hands for a couple of days, giving up his room in the cottage to his sister. He'd been staying with his mom for the last few weeks while the upstairs rooms in the main house were painted and the new flooring went down. Their mother had turned the third bedroom in the cottage into a craft room a couple of years earlier, and he wasn't about to let his baby sister sleep on the couch.

He showered and dressed, dismissing the idea of a suit and settling on dark jeans, a white shirt and a jacket. Suits and ties were not his thing. Sure, Valene was a sophisticated and educated woman, but Jake wasn't about to become someone he wasn't to impress her. He was a rancher, a cowboy, more at home in his Stetson and denim than hand-tailored suits. He kept the suits for business and the denim for pleasure.

And a date with Valene Fortunado was definitely about pleasure.

For two long days he'd been thinking about her, remembering her lovely brown eyes and the perfectly shaped mouth he was hopeful he'd get to kiss at some point.

He drove the Sierra, despite some misgivings, and had to park down the street from the restaurant because the vehicle was so big. Toscano's was a nice place, well regarded and hard to get a reservation at. But he'd been there a lot, with Patrice when they were married and many times for business lunches and for dinner. The owner, Serge, knew him, since the Double Rock supplied their beef, and he'd been happy to make a reservation for Jake.

Jake lingered by the door a few minutes to seven and felt relief pitch in his chest when he saw Valene's familiar-looking Lexus pull into a newly vacant parking space down the block. He met her by the driver's side and closed the door once she got out.

"Evening," he said and held out his hand.

Her fingers curled around his and she met his gaze. It was dark, and a chilly February night, but he felt the connection between them instantly. She wore a long coat, and her beautiful hair was down and framed her face. She was, he thought, as lovely as he remembered. Attraction skittered down his spine, and he experienced an unusual shortness of breath. It had been a long time since he had been so aware of a woman. Too long. And he liked the sensation that being around her evoked. It made him feel as though he was alive, and not the version of himself he'd allowed to take the lead since Patrice had left.

"Hello, Jake, it's nice to see you again."

"Likewise, Valene."

She smiled and withdrew her hand. "You can call me Val."

"I kinda like Valene," he admitted and waited until she'd moved onto the sidewalk before discreetly placing a hand beneath her elbow and ushering her toward the restaurant. "Is that okay?"

She smiled. "Only my dad calls me Valene. And Glammy."

"Glammy?"

She nodded and suddenly looked a little sad. "She was my grandmother. When we were kids, my sister Schuyler had a lisp and couldn't say Grammy…so the word Glammy sort of stuck. She died last year."

"I'm sorry."

"Thank you. She was a wonderful woman. One of a kind. I miss her a lot. How did you manage to get a table?" she asked as they reached the door, changing the subject. "Did you bribe the maître d'?"

He smiled and led her inside, speaking close to her ear. "Something like that."

Once they were inside, she took off her coat to reveal a stunning black-and-white dress that was modest but enhanced her lovely curves. It took about ten seconds for them to be seated and for Serge to seek Jake out. The owner, a Sicilian in his late sixties, greeted him with a friendly handshake.

"So good to see you again, Jake. It's been too long. I saved the best table for you."

Jake could only agree and figured the restaurateur had probably shuffled reservations around to give them the table situated between the small front window and the bar that was away from other diners and offered plenty of privacy.

"Thank you, Serge," he said and then introduced Valene.

The rakish Sicilian grasped Valene's hand and kissed her knuckles. "A pleasure, lovely lady. I have seen you here before, yes?"

She nodded and briefly met Jake's gaze. "Yes, mostly for business lunches. However," she said and smiled warmly, "I have never sat at the *best* table before."

The older man gave a flirtatious laugh. "Ha…nothing is too good for my friend Jake. I shall leave you the wine list and come back soon."

Once Serge left, Valene stared at Jake, brows up questioningly. "So...how?"

"How what?"

"How did you get to be on a first-name basis with the owner of one of the most popular restaurants in the city?"

Jake perused the wine list for a second and then met her inquiring gaze. "I told you I work on a ranch. It supplies the beef for the restaurant. Serge is simply a satisfied customer. Good beef equals the good table."

Her mouth curled at the edges. "You're full of surprises."

Yeah, he thought, to a woman like Valene Fortunado, it would seem like that.

And then he wondered how she'd react if he told her that the beef the Double Rock Ranch supplied to the restaurant actually belonged to him. Because everything on the ranch—the house, the stables, the cattle, the horses—was his, and had been since he'd bought the place eight years earlier.

Chapter Three

Yes...he is as gorgeous as I remember.

Valene couldn't think of anything else as she watched him look over the wine list. She wasn't sure she'd ever seen eyes his color before. They were an old movie-star blue—deep and glittering and framed by the most unfairly long lashes she'd ever seen on a man. And he smelled so good—not some fancy and expensively over-powering and cloying cologne, but a woodsy, totally masculine scent that was wreaking havoc on her dormant libido.

Sex...

How long had it been since she'd thought about sex in any real terms? A long time. Even when she was with Hugh, their relationship had been so lukewarm she rarely gave intimacy a thought. But right now, sitting opposite Jake, admiring his broad shoulders and bed-room eyes, she was suddenly thinking about it. Big-time.

"Do you have a wine preference?" he asked, looking at her over the list.

She shrugged lightly. "I prefer white."

He nodded, and within seconds Serge returned and Jake ordered a vintage from the Mendoza Winery. She wondered if he knew of her connection with the family and then figured it didn't matter. He could easily find out her background by going online. She had several social media accounts and often posted frivolous things about food and clothes and the latest pair of must-have shoes she'd purchased. It certainly wouldn't be difficult to trace her family tree and figure out she came from the Fortune family. A very rich family. Maddie's warning suddenly pealed inside her head. *Don't go too fast. Don't trust too easily.*

A waitress arrived and handed them a couple of menus. Valene was looking over the selection when he spoke.

"Everything okay, Valene?"

She looked up and nodded. "Fine. So, what's good here?"

"The beef," he replied and grinned. "Although I may be a little biased."

Valene chose the ravioli and pursed her lips. "I shall take you to task if it's inferior to my palate."

He chuckled at her playful banter. "I look forward to it."

The waitress returned with the wine and to take their order, and once they were alone, Valene spoke again. "So, Jake, have you ever had your heart broken?"

His gaze narrowed fractionally. "Yes. You?"

"Sort of."

He gave her a quizzical look. "Sort of?"

She shrugged. "Not broken…just cracked a little. It

turned out my first boyfriend, Diego, was more interested in courting my father than me."

He sat back. "Well, I can assure you that your father isn't my type."

Valene laughed. He had a lovely sense of humor and she was discovering that she liked that quality very much. "I'll have you know that my dad is very charming."

He chuckled. "I'll take your word for it."

"And he's a good judge of character," she added and sipped her wine. "He saw through Diego long before I did."

"It's good he's there to watch out for you."

"Or smother me," she said and sighed. "My parents can be a little…overprotective."

"You're their youngest child, correct?" he asked.

"Yes."

"Natural then," he said quietly, "that they would want to protect you from jerks and gold diggers."

"I suppose," she said and sighed. "And I shouldn't complain about being loved so much, I know. Tell me about your parents."

He shrugged loosely. "Not much to tell. My parents had a happy marriage. My mom never found anyone else after my father died."

"He was the love of her life?" Val suggested, thinking how wonderful it would be to feel such devotion for someone.

"I guess he was. She works three days a week at the local elementary school and has a small circle of friends. She's happy enough, I suppose. What about your mom?" he asked, turning the conversation back to her.

"My mother's name is Barbara. She and my dad love

one another like crazy. She works in a charity organization that helps women and children. I've always envied the way she can do that."

"Do what?" he inquired.

Val pressed her lips together for a moment. "Help people unselfishly. Without an agenda. She was never overly ambitious for a career—I guess my dad made up for that. But she always seems to be the best version of herself. Maybe doing things for other people makes a person their authentic best."

"I'm sure it does," Jake said evenly. "But I think when we're young, most of us are wrapped up in ourselves. It's not a character flaw…just part of growing up. Don't be too hard on yourself, Valene, I'm sure you do more for others than you realize."

Val stared at him. There was something about the rich timbre of his voice that soothed her. It also occurred to her that he wasn't the roughneck that men who worked the land were often assumed to be.

"You know, you're very…nice," she said and drank some wine. "You said you'd had your heart broken. Will you tell me about it?"

His gaze didn't waver. "There's not much to tell. We went to high school together but weren't in the same crowd. A few years after school we met up again. I loved her. I thought she loved me in return. I was mistaken. We split up."

Val knew there had to be more to the story, but she wasn't going to pry any deeper. They barely knew one another, and she had to respect his privacy. If he wanted to say more about it, he would.

Their meals arrived, and for the following hour, Valene was entertained by Jake's quiet humor and easy conversation. They talked about movies and music; he entertained her with stories about working on the ranch and she did the same with tales of selling houses and dealing with clients. She told him about Maddie and Zach's rivalry and how they fell in love. She talked about Schuyler's whirlwind romance with one of the Mendozas, and he didn't flinch at the mention of anyone's name. If he knew of her connection to the Mendozas or the Fortunes, he had a great poker face.

"Do you enjoy selling houses?" he asked once their plates had been cleared away and she was perusing the dessert menu.

Valene nodded. "Yes. But I travel a lot between Houston and Austin at the moment and the hours can be long. Not as long as yours, I imagine, from sunrise to sunset. But I often work weekends doing open houses or catching up on paperwork. In fact, I'm working tomorrow morning for a few hours."

"What's your favorite part of your job?"

She let out a long breath. "My favorite part is when I show someone a house and they have that 'this is the one' look on their face. The funny thing is, sometimes the house they finally choose is nothing like what they were originally looking for."

"I imagine it's a competitive industry."

"Fiercely," she replied. "Even among people working in the same office. Landing an exclusive listing is so important but often difficult in today's climate. Different agents offer different incentives, but I try not to get wrapped up in the theatrics. I simply match up my listing and prospective buyers the best I can. I mean, buying property is a *considered* purchase, not something people do on a whim. So I get to know the clients as real people. Their history, their family, their dreams. Buying a home is usually the biggest financial commitment someone will make in their lifetime, so I try to make the experience as stress-free as possible."

As she spoke, she longed to feel a surge of passion for what she did. Val liked her job. But she didn't *love* it. She enjoyed working in the family business and strove to be the best she could be. She wasn't as ambitious as Maddie and had little interest in climbing the corporate ladder or being in charge, but the selling, the brokering of deals, the influence she had when she clinched a sale, were challenging and had their rewards.

"I imagine you're very good at getting people to trust you," he remarked, sipping his wine.

Val smiled. "I'd like to think so. And you're right, my clients, both buyers and sellers, put a lot of trust in my hands. So I'm always up front about what the home is worth, how it presents, how it feels. And I believe they appreciate that. Honesty is the key."

His blue eyes glittered brilliantly. "You're right. And since we're on the subject of honesty, I should come clean and tell you that I never order dessert."

Val smiled. "Well, I don't see how this is ever going to work, then."

There was something hypnotic about his gaze, and she couldn't have dragged her eyes away from his even if she'd wanted to. With every look, every word, Valene felt herself getting dragged further into his vortex.

"You can order dessert if you want," he told her. "I hear the cheesecake is good."

She shook her head. "I like my sweets in the morning. There's this place down the road from my office, the Moon Beam Bakery, that does the most amazing blueberry and cream cheese bagels." She moaned her delight.

"So, then, instead of dessert, would you like to go dancing?" he asked.

Oh, God, he danced, too.

The man was perfect. Well, except for every other way that he wasn't. The clothes, although neat and well fitted, were cowboy garb, and of course there was his beat-up truck and the fact he was a ranch hand. But still…he really was incredibly attractive. And smart. And funny.

She nodded. "I would."

"Let's go."

He signaled the waitress, paid the check with a credit card and said a quick farewell to Serge before helping her into her coat. It was chilly outside, and she pulled up the collar around her neck.

"Where are we going?" she asked as they stepped onto the sidewalk.

"Just down the block," he replied. "Are you happy to walk or would you prefer we drive?"

She looked down at her pointy shoes and nodded, thinking that Maddie would blow a gasket if she agreed to get into a car with a man she barely knew. But Valene didn't feel as though she was in any danger with Jake. There was something unwaveringly trustworthy about him. He possessed an aura of enviable integrity, as though it was ingrained within his DNA.

Still, it was such a short distance, she opted to walk.

He grasped her elbow, and even through the woolen coat, she could feel the heat coming off his skin. They walked down the block and then across the road, passing several couples along the way before they reached their destination. She'd been anticipating the fashionable jazz club a few doors down from where they stood. But no. This wasn't the jazz place.

Valene came to an abrupt halt once she heard the music emanating from the very country, very cowboy bar and grill. Of course, she'd passed the place many times, but she had never ventured through the doors of the Red Elk. It was honky-tonk style, with a bar and booth seats and a dance floor toward the back. The place was surprisingly subdued and nowhere near as rowdy and noisy as she'd imagined.

"Ah... I don't really know how to dance to cowboy songs," she said as he ushered her through the doorway and toward a table near the dance floor.

He was smiling. "It's easy," he replied and took her coat, hanging it over the back of a chair. "You just hold on and sway."

Val wasn't convinced. There were a few other couples on the dance floor, and the song changed just as Jake took her hand. Electricity rushed up her arm and she was sure her cheeks spotted with color. And then like magic, she was in his arms. He didn't grope her, didn't do anything other than hold her one hand and then place his other respectfully at her waist. Val reached up and placed her hand on his shoulder and then followed his lead. Of course, he knew what he was doing, and slow dancing clearly came to him as easily as breathing. And the song, a romantic Brett Young number, was exactly the right kind of melody for the mood she was in.

He might be a penniless cowboy, but Jake Brockton knew how to dance. In fact, she was pretty sure he was one of those men who mastered everything he did. And then, of course, she knew he'd be a spectacular kisser. Which was why she looked up, her lips parted slightly as she met his gaze, her eyes clearly betraying her.

Because what she wanted in that moment, more than anything, was his mouth on hers, and she was absolutely certain that he knew it!

* * *

Jake had never in his life wanted to kiss anyone as much as he wanted to kiss Valene Fortunado. Of course, he wouldn't. But he was tempted. It didn't help that her slumberous chocolate-brown eyes were regarding him with seductive invitation. Or that every time she moved, her lovely curves brushed against him.

But it was too soon.

He liked her. He liked her a lot. More than he'd been prepared for when he'd asked her out to dinner. Or suggested they go dancing. But Jake wasn't a hasty man. And even though Valene was delightful and beautiful, he had to show some sense and some self-control.

"See," he said easily, ignoring the way his heart was beating, "you *can* dance to a cowboy song."

She smiled. "I'm just swaying."

"That's all you gotta do, sweetheart."

She smiled again, and the expression reached him way down low. It had been forever since he'd danced with a woman, and he'd forgotten how much he liked it. There was something intoxicating about the way they moved together, and he suspected she felt it, too. Valene was unashamedly honest and the knowledge caused a jolt of shame to slice between his shoulder blades. He needed to come clean, to tell her the truth about himself. But his resistance lingered. He'd already had one woman rip his heart out—he wasn't ready to allow someone else in to do the same. Not just yet.

And he didn't want to ruin the mood or change the dynamic of the evening. He liked that she hadn't made a big deal about his life or occupation. He liked that she hadn't balked outside the honky-tonk and refused to go inside, even though he was sure she'd never set foot in a place like it before. She had gumption and spine and was a strong, independent woman, probably stronger than she knew.

They danced for a while, all slow numbers that suited him and the mood that had developed between them. When the music finally changed to an upbeat number, he took her hand and led her back to their table.

"There are peanut shells on the floor," she remarked when he returned with a drink for them both, light beer for him and bottled water for her.

"It's a cowboy bar," he said and smiled. "Goes with the territory."

"Until someone slips on a shell and then sues the proprietor."

Jake watched her over the rim of his glass. "That wouldn't happen."

"Cowboy code, huh?" she suggested, brows up a little.

"I guess you could call it that. You know, we're not so different from you city folk. We eat, dance, make love…do all the things that the urban dwellers do."

She smiled so sexily he had to shift in his seat. Damn, she was hot.

"That's reassuring," she said quietly and unscrewed the lid off her drink. "We've mastered two out of three."

She was flirting. Unabashedly and provocatively. And Jake was so turned on he could have hauled her into his arms and kissed her without hesitation.

"You're very beautiful, Valene," he said quietly. "Probably more than you know. But I'm not going to rush into anything, okay?"

He felt like a conceited fool for saying it…but he wanted the air clear between them. He didn't want her thinking he was some randy cowboy who simply wanted to get laid and have a little fun. Well, of course he wanted to have fun, and he wanted to get laid…but he also wanted to get to know her. The real Valene Fortunado. Not just the sweet, if somewhat spoiled, party-girl image she had on social media. He'd checked her out, of course, having no choice once he'd told Cassidy who she was. His sister had brought up page after page of highlights from Valene's life and lifestyle and forced Jake to take a look.

He wondered if she'd done the same. He didn't have any personal social media accounts, but if she dug a little deeper, she'd find him easily enough, through articles and interviews and local business affiliations. Valene was a smart and resourceful woman, and it occurred to Jake that she might know exactly who he was, and all about his portfolio and net worth. It unnerved him a little, since she'd bleated on about honesty and transparency. But he didn't think she was underhanded. On the other hand, he hadn't believed Patrice was a liar or a cheat, either—until his life and marriage spectacularly blew up in his face.

"Okay," she said softly. "To be honest, Jake, I'm not the rushing type. I don't jump into bed with every man I meet."

He knew that, of course. There was a sweetness and an innocence about Valene that simmered underneath the surface. And she was young, just twenty-four. Plus, she'd clearly been protected and watched over all her life. He was glad about that, hating to think that she'd ever suffered adversity or real heartbreak.

"Then we agree…slow is best?"

She nodded and smiled in a way that made his insides contract. "Sure…just not *too* slow, okay, Jake?"

Laughter rumbled in his chest, and he spent the next half hour listening to her talk about dancing, the best places to get coffee in town, her beloved dog, and her close relationship with her sisters and how much she missed them since one had moved to Austin to be with the man she loved, and the other had recently married and commuted between Houston and Austin.

"Maddie and Zach are the perfect couple," she said. "He gets her need to be in charge of everything and everyone, and even though he's as business focused as she is, he has a good sense of fun. And Carlo and Schuyler are perfect for one another, too. He knows how to deal with her craziness. All my siblings are either married or engaged now...well, except for Connor. I think he's determined to *never* fall in love."

"What about you?" he asked, knowing her answer even before she replied. But caution told him that Valene Fortunado might be in love with the idea of being in love.

"Of course I want to be in love," she replied. "But I don't want it to be too distracting. With everything that's going on with the family business, I need to stay focused."

"Is something wrong with your business?" he asked, his gaze narrowing.

She shrugged, looking as though she'd said too much. "Nothing we can't handle."

"Big business can be tough."

She nodded. "But I like the challenge. And Maddie is giving me more opportunity to shine, which is great. In fact, she and Zach have recently let me take the lead on signing a really important client. Which we need."

Jake backed off, but he made a mental note to do a little investigating. From all accounts, the Fortunado family was wealthy and successful. If that was a facade, he figured he needed to know before he got in any deeper with Valene.

"You father is a self-made man, I presume?" he asked quietly.

She shrugged. "Kind of. He was lucky enough to have had a lottery win some years ago. He invested wisely, made a few good decisions and started the real estate business. The business grew, and we now have offices in San Antonio and Austin as well as Houston."

It occurred to Jake that Kenneth Fortunado was much like himself. Jake had invested the sum he'd inherited from his father's life insurance, plus the money he'd earned working at the ranch and also packing shelves at Mason's Minimart just outside Fulshear. Five years later he had enough to make an offer when the ranch came up for sale. A few years and some sound business decisions later, including his investment in the lucrative Wagyu beef market, and he owned the ranch outright and had more money in the bank than he could ever spend.

"You admire him a lot?"

She nodded. "I admire people who make their dreams come true. My dad did that and created a legacy that will continue to grow. My sister Maddie is now CEO alongside her husband, so the business is in good hands."

"And what are your ambitions?"

"To be the best I can be," she replied. "At whatever I do. When I graduated college, I went directly into the business and haven't regretted it. I enjoy the work and get to spend my days helping people find the home of their dreams. It's a win-win."

Jake realized he could easily get hooked on her passion for life. She was definitely a glass-half-full kind of girl. He liked that about her. The truth was, he liked everything about her.

They stayed for a little while longer, but by ten she

said she'd had enough. Jake helped her into her coat and then walked her from the bar and back down the street. Once they reached her car, she fished inside her small bag for her keys and unlocked the vehicle.

"Well, thank you for a lovely evening," she said and held out her hand.

He stared down into her face, watching as her mouth parted slightly and his own mouth tingled in response. She was eminently kissable. But he wasn't about to have his first kiss with Valene Fortunado in the middle of a busy street with people walking past.

He took her hand and enclosed his fingers around hers. "Good night, Valene. I'll call you."

"Are you sure?" she asked quietly, almost nervously.

"Positive."

She nodded fractionally. "Okay, see you soon."

As she stepped into the car and drove off down the street, Jake remained on the sidewalk, hands on his hips, staring after the fading taillights. And he knew one thing. He fully intended on seeing Valene again.

And the sooner, the better.

Chapter Four

Two dates. Two really enjoyable interactions. Good company. Dancing. And not one kiss.

So maybe Jake wasn't interested in her in that way. Perhaps he wasn't attracted to her and had put her in the friend zone. Maybe she had misread the connection they appeared to have. It wouldn't be the first time she'd been misled by a man's intentions, after all.

When Val arrived home, Bruce greeted her with slobbery enthusiasm and bounded around her feet. Her ground-floor condo had a small garden and Bruce had a doggy door to come and go, but he mostly spent his days curled up on the couch or sprawled in the middle of her bed. Perhaps it was just as well she wasn't sharing the sheets with anyone, she thought and laughed to herself. It would certainly put Bruce's nose out of joint if she did.

She started humming the Brett Young tune as she

slipped off her dress and shoes and put on her pajamas. She cleaned off her makeup, brushed her teeth, slathered on hand cream and sat on the edge of her bed, thinking, wondering.

Okay…so Jake didn't find her particularly attractive, that had to be it. And he was too polite to say anything. Although he had said she was pretty *and* called her "sweetheart." And he didn't look at her as though she was in the friends-only category. Val was certain she'd seen attraction and awareness in his eyes. He had said he wanted to go slow. And she'd agreed.

Then why am I making a big deal out of him not kissing me good-night?

Because she'd wanted to kiss him, that's why.

She'd wanted to feel his arms around her and his mouth on hers. She was achingly attracted to him, even though she knew he was nothing like the kind of man she'd convinced herself was right for her. She'd wanted to find someone as driven and ambitious as Zach, or as charming and sophisticated as Carlo. Someone from her world.

Perhaps Jake understood that and that's why he'd kept the evening casual. And she liked him, so maybe friendship might be enough. Or perhaps he was seeing someone else at the same time, some other woman, or women, that he met on the dating app. Of course, he could do what he wanted. Still, the notion wounded her just a little.

Val was still mulling over her predicament the following morning as she sat at her desk, half-heartedly working on a proposal for one of her clients. She hated that she was preoccupied and had tried to pull herself together since she'd arrived at the office an hour earlier. But she was in a funk. And it was all Jake Brockton's fault. That, and a disappointing email she'd received from her sister that she kept reading over and over.

"Got a minute?" said a voice, and then Maddie stuck her head around the door.

Val look up from her computer, saw that Maddie had a furrow between her brows and nodded. "Sure."

"Did you get the email I sent you?" she asked. "About the Waterson estate?"

The owner of the estate was now deceased, and every agent in Houston had been vying for the opportunity to sell the mansion and the three commercial properties the owner had left to his only grandson, a young man who resided in California and had no interest in living on the estate. Val had spent weeks talking with the man, and a week earlier he'd committed to listing the places with Fortunado Real Estate. At least, that's what she'd believed...until Maddie had forwarded his email, informing the office that he'd decided to go with someone else, a firm that was their biggest competitor. A firm she believed had no scruples and that certainly didn't offer the service her family's company did. It was a big blow. Maddie and Zach had entrusted the client to her, and she felt as though she had seriously let them down.

"I don't know what happened." She shrugged. "It was all going well. I have the contracts almost ready to go. I've booked photographers and stylists for a shoot. I just..." Her words trailed off and she shrugged again. "I can't explain it."

"Are you sure?"

Val frowned. "What does that mean?"

"You've been distracted this week," Maddie said bluntly. "You've had that cowboy on your mind for days."

Val tried to keep a lid on her temper. She loved Maddie, and her sister wasn't being deliberately mean, but she had a responsibility to the firm, and Val understood she needed to ask the tough questions.

"This has nothing to do with Jake," she defended quietly.

"It's the second deal you've had go sour this week," Maddie reminded her, and Val quickly recalled the other owner who'd pulled a listing. "And the only thing that is different from last week to this one is your new boyfriend."

"He's not my boyfriend," Val stated firmly. "We've been on two dates. If you must know, he hasn't even tried to kiss me. So, I'm not distracted. I'm no different than I was last week or last month. And I can't explain why I've lost two listings this week. I'm so sorry about the Waterson deal. I know it would have meant a lot to the firm. I can call him and—"

"No point." Maddie waved a hand. "Zach put through a call early this morning, and it doesn't look as though the owner will change his mind. He said he was going with a firm who had a more *experienced* team. If Zach couldn't talk this around, no one can. We've lost this one, Val. I'd like you to start running things by Zach again, like you used to."

Val's insides hurt. Her sister looked so disappointed in her and she had no words of explanation to offer, no excuses or justification for what had happened. She'd bombed, big-time. And she didn't blame Maddie for being annoyed. But it hurt. Her big sister's approval had always been important to her, especially since Maddie had become her boss.

She waited until her sister left her office and then let out a long and painful sigh, resting her face in her hands. What a mess. Missing out on the Waterson deal was a huge loss. The commission and kudos would have been so good for the business. And for her. Now she felt like a monumental failure.

"Everything okay, Valene?"

She knew that voice. It had haunted her dreams the night before. Val looked up and spotted Jake standing in the doorway, a small brown bag in one hand, a take-out coffee cup in the other. She hadn't expected to see him, and it was a delightful surprise.

Her breath shuddered. "What are you doing here?" she asked and straightened immediately.

He took a few steps into the room. "I had a few things to do in town." He dropped the brown bag on her desk. "Blueberry cream cheese bagel. And a low-fat, single-shot, extra cinnamon vanilla soy latte," he said and placed the coffee by the computer. "From your favorite bakery."

Val let out a long sigh, touched that he'd remembered. "Thank you. How did you know how to find me?"

"The receptionist at the front desk," he supplied. "And last night you said you were working for a few hours this morning. I knew the location of the office and took my chances, hoping you'd still be here. But next time I can call first if you prefer."

Val didn't prefer. She was very happy to see him. She got to her feet, wrapping her fingers around the coffee, and took a sip. "You can stop by anytime you like. And thank you. I needed to see a friendly face."

His gaze narrowed. "Bad morning?"

"The worst." She briefly explained about losing the account and then backpedaled a little because she knew she probably shouldn't be talking about the family business to a man she hardly knew. "Sorry... I didn't mean to vent."

He smiled. "No problem. Actually, the reason I'm here is I was wondering if you were free tomorrow?"

Tomorrow. Sunday. If she had any sense, she would tell him she had work to do, reports to catch up on, plans to make about how to reel the Waterson deal back in. But it *was* Sunday. And all work and no play was no way to function.

Plus, he looked so damned appealing in his jeans, beige chambray shirt and sheepskin-lined jacket. And the fact that he'd brought her the coffee and bagel she liked…well, she couldn't be blamed for being a little smitten with him.

"Free for what?" she asked him.

His gaze narrowed a fraction, and she wondered if he'd picked up in the flirtation in her reply. He smiled then, and she saw that he had. "I thought we could spend the morning together."

It sounded like a great idea, and she was just about to say so when her sister Schuyler walked into the office. One thing about her crazy sibling, she had impeccable timing. Not.

"Oh, sorry," Schuyler gushed and quickly gave the man standing by her desk a deliberate once-over. "Didn't mean to interrupt."

Val raised a brow. "This is Jake. This is my sister Schuyler. She lives in Austin and is leaving soon, right?"

Schuyler chuckled and shook Jake's hand. "Tomorrow morning. Carlo is back from his business thing tomorrow and I want to be home when he returns. We're still newlyweds," she told Jake with a wicked grin, and Val envied her sister's ability to sound so effortlessly flirtatious. "I miss him madly. And my baby sister is right. But I just wanted to remind you about dinner tonight with me and Maddie. Unless," she added and gave Jake another long and deliberate perusal, "you have other plans."

Val waved her hand. "I'll see you tonight. At seven. *Goodbye*, Schuyler." Once her sister left, Val let out a long sigh. "Sorry about that. My sister is—"

"Probably as annoying as mine," he said, cutting her off and smiling. "But that's why we love 'em, right?"

Val laughed. "Absolutely. I adore Schuyler. She's like this force of nature and has incredibly positive energy."

"You're not so different," he remarked.

Val's insides crunched up. How often had she envied her sister's ability to remain a free spirit but stay true to who she was? Like she'd also sought to be more like Maddie—focused and completely on track with her life.

Her cell beeped with a text, and she excused herself for a moment as she was expecting a message from a client who had a showing on Monday. But it wasn't a client. It was Schuyler.

OMG! He's so hot. Who cares if he doesn't have two pennies to rub together. Go for it, kid!

Val's skin burned. Trust her sister to say exactly what she was thinking.

"Sorry," she said and put down the phone. "So, you were saying something about tomorrow?"

He nodded. "I'll pick you up around nine, unless that's too early?"

"No," she replied. "I'm a morning person. I rarely sleep past six."

"Something else we have in common."

She liked that notion. "I imagine your work demands

an early start. I usually hit the treadmill for half an hour in the morning. Or hang out with my dog, Bruce."

He nodded. "You told me about him last night. I'm glad you like dogs."

"I like cats, too," she admitted. "But it's more challenging to take a cat for a walk in the park."

He laughed, and the lovely sound filled her with a silly kind of happiness. She liked that she could make him laugh.

"Okay, I'll pick you up at nine, as long as you text me your address. Or I can meet you somewhere in town."

Val thought about it for a moment. She could take the safe road and meet him on neutral ground. But nothing about Jake felt threatening to her. "You can pick me up. I'll text you."

He half smiled. "Okay. Oh, and wear something comfortable."

Once he left, Val got her mind back to work. She left around lunchtime, grabbing a few groceries on the way home. She did some much-needed housework in the afternoon and arrived at Maddie and Zach's home just before seven. They also rented a place in Austin, but she knew her sister enjoyed spending weekends in their hometown. Schuyler was already there, legs dangling over the edge of a counter stool in the kitchen, sipping on a margarita.

Val declined the alcohol, preferring club soda, which Zach poured for her just before he announced he had work to do and would be tucked away in his office well out of the way of their girl time.

"So, I was just telling Maddie how sexy your cowboy is," Schuyler said with a wicked chuckle.

"Please don't," Val protested. "She already thinks I'm distracted from my work."

"There's more to life than work, ladies," Schuyler said and gave them both a playful grin. "There's fun and friendship and...sex. Which Maddie here knows all about since she hooked up with our gorgeous brother-in-law. And I absolutely forbid us to talk about work tonight."

Val met Maddie's gaze. "I'm sorry about the Waterson deal," she said, ignoring Schuyler's protest.

"I know," Maddie said gently. "And I'm not angry. *Or* disappointed. I do want you to be happy, Val. I'm not saying you shouldn't have a social life...you absolutely should. Just tread carefully. You don't know anything about this guy."

I know he's handsome and charming and considerate and nice...and sexy.

"Okay," she said quietly, knowing Maddie wouldn't give up her lioness mode. "I'll tread carefully. I promise."

"He really is ridiculously good-looking," Schuyler sighed. "So, where's he taking you tomorrow?"

Val shrugged. "I have no idea. He simply said to wear something casual."

Maddie frowned. "Like sweats kind of casual, or jeans and a Calvin Klein T-shirt casual?"

"I was thinking I'd go for something in between," she replied and grinned.

"Maybe he's taking you horseback riding?" Schuyler suggested. "Isn't that what cowboys do in their spare time? A nice, long, romantic ride on that ranch he works at. You know, if you tell me his last name, I will happily snoop on the internet and find out everything there is to know about him."

"No," Val said firmly. "I don't want to start out that way."

"Safety first," Maddie said wryly. "You should be more cautious. What if he takes you to some isolated spot and—"

"Oh, for heaven's sake, he's not an ax murderer," Val responded, her irritation rising. "And stop smothering me."

"Mom and Dad asked me to look out for you while they were away," Maddie said matter-of-factly. "If they knew you were seeing someone you met off a dating app, they would blow a gasket."

"Um, wasn't it your idea?" Val reminded her sister.

Maddie hooked a thumb in Schuyler's direction. "Her idea. I didn't think you'd actually go through with it."

"We can't all meet the man of our dreams in the workplace," she said and smiled sweetly. "And leave Mom and Dad out of this. They're not back from their trip for another couple of weeks."

"Plenty of time for you to get into trouble."

"Ha. I'm not interested in trouble."

"But you are interested in this cowboy," Maddie said flatly. "Even though he is nothing like the kind of man you said you wanted."

Val shrugged. "So…maybe I've changed my mind about what I want."

"He could be a player, or some kind of heartless philanderer."

Val laughed so loud she snorted. "Seriously, have you been reading Brontë and Austen again?" She looked toward Schuyler and raised both hands. "Do something, will you?"

Schuyler grinned. "She doesn't listen to me."

"I just think you need to be careful," Maddie said, still serious. "With everything that has been going on, we can't be too careful."

Everything...

Val knew what she meant. Losing contracts at Fortunado Real Estate was one thing, but there had been other signs that things were awry. Like the fact that Robinson Tech had recently been hacked and an attempt had been made to sabotage their operating systems. Or worse—the fire at the Robinson estate and the even more disturbing fact that their cousin Ben Fortune Robinson had almost been killed. Yes, things had been happening. Unexplained things. But Val had no reason to suspect that her meeting Jake was in any way connected to these events. Val stared at one sister, then the other, thinking that neither truly understood how she felt. Of course, she took stock of Maddie's warnings, but she was also keen to adopt Schuyler's philosophy about embracing life.

And she figured that hanging out with Jake Brockton was doing exactly that.

Jake whistled under his breath when he pulled up outside Val's luxury condo in the River Oaks district. It was a high-end spot, one of the best in the city, and he let the engine run on the Ranger but put it in Park and got out, waiting for her by the security gate. The complex was one of many that had risen in the city in the past decade and was designed to be hurricane-proof. There was a small pond and several bench seats and an abundance of trees and gardens behind the tall fence.

Val appeared a couple of minutes later, in jeans, a bright red shirt, knee-high boots and a fitted dark jacket. Her hair was down and she smiled as she greeted him, allowing the gate to lock automatically behind her. She looked beautiful and vibrant and so enticing he could barely stop himself from staring at her like an enraptured fool.

"Hi there," she said cheerfully.

"Good morning. Nice spot," he said and opened the passenger door.

She smiled, and his insides flipped over. "When I moved out, my dad insisted I relocate to a gated community for security reasons. This place came up, and he pitched in so I could afford it."

Jake's brows rose. "Pitched in?"

She shrugged. "Okay…so he pitched in the whole amount. But I fully intend to pay him back one day. And he got the place for a song because it was part of an ugly divorce."

Jake's back straightened. He knew all about bitter divorces. He'd had the worst breakup of the century. And Val's flippant reaction to something so emotionally devastating stung a little. But she was young. Probably too young for him. And probably, as he had suspected from their first meeting, more in love with the idea of being in love than wanting a real and messy relationship.

It should have registered on his radar.

But being around her, sharing molecules of space with her, was inexplicably soothing. Which was at odds with the blistering attraction he felt for her. It was a heady mix of lust and like, something he couldn't remember experiencing before. And for a man who only a few days ago had firmly denied he'd get seriously involved with anyone, he knew he was stupidly backpedaling.

"Let's go."

She got in the truck, dropped her tote between her feet and buckled up. "I think this rig is older than me," she said when he got in.

Jake half smiled. "A second-class drive is better than a first-class walk."

She laughed loudly and fiddled with the magnetic religious medal attached to the center console. "That's so true. What's this?"

"Saint Eligius," he replied.

"Who?"

"Patron saint of horses."

She looked impressed. "Are you an expert on the saints?"

"Not all," he replied and grinned. "I'm not sure I'm an expert on anything. What about you? Do you have a particular talent?"

She looked directly ahead. "Well, I recently learned how to dance cowboy style. And I know how to order a fancy cup of coffee."

"That's quite a skill."

"I know," she said and laughed. "I am envied in several states."

God, she was intoxicating. He couldn't recall ever being as aware of a woman as he was of Valene. The perfume she wore, something flowery and subtle, touched his senses and he inhaled discreetly, allowing the memory of the fragrance to linger in his brain like a rush of endorphins.

Jake pulled away from the sidewalk and turned the vehicle south, heading out of the city.

"Where are we going?" she asked. "I need to let my sister know, otherwise she's going to worry all morning. Maddie can be overprotective."

He quickly told her the address. "Understandable. I'd probably demand Cassidy do exactly the same thing. Older siblings tend to think they have to do all of the protecting. But I promise you, Valene, I'm not a threat to you."

"I know that," she said and sent a quick text. "Can I ask you something?"

His chest tightened, thinking perhaps she'd discovered he wasn't exactly who he'd said he was. "Of course."

She took a sharp breath. "Are you...are you doing this with anyone else?"

"This?" he echoed and then quickly realized her meaning. "I don't—"

"I know," she said and waved a dismissive hand. "You don't have to explain yourself to me. I mean, this is only our third date and I have no claim on your time. I mean, this is just a friends thing for you, right? And it's not like you're attracted to me or anything, and so I understand if you want to see other—"

"Valene," Jake said quietly, cutting off her impassioned speech, his gaze directly on the road ahead. "I'm not seeing anyone else, I assure you. And I am definitely attracted to you."

He heard her soft sigh. "Oh, okay."

"Are you always so nervous around men?"

Her chuckle was whisper quiet. "Actually, I think this is the least nervous I've ever been."

He smiled and relaxed a little. Despite her bravado, despite her enthusiasm for life and her delightful sense of humor, there was an earnestness about Valene that he found incredibly alluring. Sure, she was probably a little spoiled and definitely overprotected, but there was nothing deliberately arrogant or condescending about her. Even her trite remark about the truck had been more humorous than insulting. And despite what she knew about him—or rather, didn't know—she appeared to genuinely want to pursue something between them.

"I won't ever deliberately hurt you, Valene, not physically or emotionally. I've been there, and it's a dark place."

Her head turned. "You mean your last relationship?"

He nodded. "Yep. It ended badly."

"If you ever want to talk about it," she said softly, "you can."

Jake shrugged. He'd stopped talking about Patrice because the memories of all she had put him through, and all he had lost, made him ache inside. "I know. And thank you. One day, okay?"

"Sure," she replied.

Jake turned the truck left and pulled into a parking lot. "We're here."

She looked around and then swiveled in her seat. "An animal shelter?"

He shrugged. "Is it okay?"

"Of course," she replied. "I'm just surprised. My sister was convinced we were going horseback riding."

He smiled, amused that he'd been the topic of conversation with her sisters. "Maybe next time."

She nodded, and he noticed that her cheeks were flushed. "So, what are we doing here? Are you looking for a puppy?"

"I volunteer here sometimes," he said, feeling faintly embarrassed by her sudden and intense scrutiny.

She smiled, nodded and quickly grabbed her tote and got out of the truck.

Jake watched her as she strolled up the path leading to the front door, actually admiring the way she didn't hang back and wait for him. Valene clearly wasn't afraid of new things.

He caught up with her and they walked through to the reception desk side by side. He'd been volunteering at the Sweet Pines Shelter since he was a teenager. It was where he'd found his first canine companion, Rudy. The old dog was long gone now, but he had fond memories of the day he'd brought him home, sitting alongside him and his dad in the same old truck that was now parked outside.

"Good morning, sunshine!"

The familiar singsong voice that greeted them belonged to Florence, a volunteer who had been working at the shelter for close to twenty years. The sixtysomething-year-old woman was the heart and soul of the shelter. Jake introduced her to Valene, and Florence was clearly intrigued.

"A girl?" Florence queried and chuckled.

"I brought supplies, too," he replied and tugged a little at his collar. "I'll drive the truck around the back and unload." He looked toward Valene. "Be back in a sec."

Jake grinned and walked back through the front door, thinking that hanging out with Valene was just about the best way to spend a Sunday morning. Unless he was spending it in her bed.

Which he figured wasn't too far off in his future, either.

Chapter Five

"He's such a sweet boy."

Valene stared at the older woman and smiled. *Boy?* Jake was about as far from a boy as you could get. But it was quite adorable that Florence thought so.

"I take it you've known Jake for a long time?" Valene asked.

She nodded. "Oh, yes, since he was a teenager. When he was young, he used to come and help tend to the animals, particularly the ones that had been abused or neglected. Of course he's so busy these days he doesn't have time to do that, but he's here without fail once a month, donating food and bedding and cat litter. And he always helps out by fixing things around the place when he's here," she added, clearly adoring him. "If I'd had a son, I'd want him to be just like Jake. Not that I'd trade my daughters for a son, but you know what I mean. There was a time when I hoped my youngest might be a good match for him," Florence said and shrugged. "But she married a house painter and moved to New Mexico. I was starting to think Jake would never find someone again after the way he got his heart broke. But," she said and gently patted Valene's arm, "I'm glad to see that he has."

"Oh, we're not—"

"He's a special man," Florence said, cutting her off gently. "But my guess is you already know that."

Valene didn't disagree and didn't try to correct the other woman again. At that moment Jake came striding down the corridor from the rear of the building and rejoined them.

"Do you mind if I whisk Valene away now?"

Florence laughed. "Of course not. And I told Digby that you were going to be here today, so he's been running around in his pen all morning."

Jake laughed and gently grasped Valene's elbow. "Catch you later, Florrie."

Florrie? Digby? Valene chuckled to herself as they walked down the corridor. The sound of dogs barking hit her ears the moment they reached the rear door. The shelter was obviously well run, clean and tidy. The dog pens were spacious and each one had a bed. And sadly, every single one had a resident locked inside.

"Jake?"

He was a couple of steps ahead, but quickly turned. "Yes?"

"Who's Digby?"

He pointed to a pen a couple of doors down and she followed him, to come face-to-face with the most adorable little dog. A mixed breed, perhaps spaniel and collie, with white and brown patches and the fluffiest feet she'd ever seen.

"This is Digby." At the sound of Jake's voice, the pooch started yelping excitedly, and when Jake opened the pen, the dog raced out and jumped around his legs. "He's a long-term resident," he explained and bent down to pick up the dog. "And an old-timer. His owner passed away and there were no relatives or neighbors to take him in. So he ended up here and has called this place home for nine months."

Valene's heart lurched. The poor little thing. And he clearly adored Jake.

"You should adopt him."

"I'd love to," he replied. "But this little guy likes to run off, and I'm afraid he might end up in all kinds of trouble if he tangled with some of the local wildlife around the ranch. Plus I'm not sure how Sheba would take to sharing the bottom of my bed." He ushered the dog back into the pen and looked at her. "I gotta unload the truck. Feel like keeping me company?"

She nodded enthusiastically. "I can help."

They passed a couple of volunteers, a pair of twenty-something women who knew Jake by name and made goo-goo eyes at him when he greeted them. It was enough to straighten Valene's spine and make her stare daggers. Thankfully, Jake seemed perfectly immune to their flirtation, intent on unloading his truck. Once they were outside, he pulled the tarp off the truck bed and Valene saw a huge pile of supplies.

"You donate this every month?" she queried, both startled and impressed by his generosity.

"More or less. Local funding doesn't quite cover the costs of the place. And it's just a small way of helping out."

"Small way?" she echoed as she stared at the supplies. "This must have cost you hundreds."

He shrugged, looking acutely embarrassed, and quickly began unloading the large bags of dog food. Valene helped with the smaller bags, stacking them in the shed, and they finished the task within ten minutes.

"What now?" she asked.

"I've got a couple of chores to do," he replied. "A few maintenance things. You can be my apprentice or hang out with Florence."

"I'd like to hang out with you," she said and smiled. "If that's okay."

"Perfectly," he said and the warmth in his voice made Valene's body heat from head to toe.

It was, she decided a couple of hours later, the most unorthodox date she had ever been on. And yet, it was surprisingly the most fun. Of course she knew that Jake was good company, but away from the standard date scenario, he was even more relaxed and funny and engaging.

And perfect boyfriend material.

It took Valene about two seconds to snap herself out of such thoughts, even if traces of the idea lingered around the edges of her mind for most of the morning.

By midday, while Jake was repairing one of the large dog runs with one of the other volunteers, who she quickly discovered was Florence's husband, Valene ended up back in the reception area, photocopying flyers for an upcoming fund-raiser.

"You're welcome to come and help us," Florence said and grinned. "Jake can bring you. It's a really fun day, and we get to do so many adoptions."

Valene was tempted, particularly since she'd witnessed three adoptions that morning—two dogs and a crazy, one-eyed ginger cat. It was delightful to watch the three separate groups choose a new family member.

She'd couldn't help feeling emotional when she watched the small child hug his new puppy, or the elderly couple who were replacing the cat they'd recently lost.

When Jake was finished with the repairs, he returned to the reception area, two coffee cups in his hands. Florence had left Val in charge of meeting and greeting, and she was having a lovely time talking to potential adopters.

Jake came around the counter and perched himself on the edge of the desk. "Everything okay?"

Valene nodded, watching the way the denim stretched over his thighs and his shirt fit across his broad shoulders. She swallowed hard, feeling the intimacy of the space between them, meeting his gaze and noticing everything about his perfectly handsome face. He had slight stubble across his jaw, as though he hadn't shaved for a day or so, and a tiny scar above his left temple. She wondered how he'd gotten that scar, just like she wondered how she'd managed to capture the attention of such a complex yet stunningly normal man. He was confident and clearly comfortable in his own skin. He didn't brag, didn't gloat, didn't name-drop or go on about his life, his work or any accomplishments. He was funny and self-effacing and had a kind of effortless charm. He was also, she realized, the polar opposite of any other man she had dated.

"I'm glad you brought me here," she said and smiled "It feels good to do something for someone else. I don't get the chance very often."

"The chance?" he queried, his gaze locked with hers.

Val sighed. "Okay, I don't *take* the opportunity. I know I should. My mother does so much for charity, particularly her work with the Fortunado Foundation.

I envy how generous she is with herself. Maybe I'd be a better person if I did more for others. Like you."

"It's not a contest, Valene," he said softly. "And perhaps it's something you could do *with* your mom. After my dad died, I spent a lot of time wishing I'd spent more time with him, made more of an effort, you know. But you can't live in the past, either. If you want to change, then change. But frankly, I think you're a very good person. You're smart and beautiful and funny and great to be around."

Val stared at him, mesmerized by the deepness of his voice and the intensity of his gaze. She wondered, briefly, if she'd ever met a man with bluer eyes, or a stronger jawline, or more innate integrity. And all she could think was no.

They left the shelter shortly after, stopping on the way to grab some lunch. They sat in a small café in the park a few streets away, eating burgers and sharing a side of fries, sitting close together at the tiny table for two. Jake had ordered them sodas and she sipped her beverage in between bites of her food.

"I've had a nice time today," she said quietly. "Thank you."

He smiled. "Anytime."

"So…does that mean you'd like to see me again?"

"Absolutely."

She was delighted to hear it, ignoring the tiny voice in her head telling her that he wasn't what she was looking for. The truth was, Valene had never come close to finding the right man. Until now. Everything about Jake *felt* right. The fact that he was a cowboy in worn denim and drove a twenty-year-old truck somehow didn't bother her one bit. She'd parted ways with Diego because he'd wanted a job, and when that hadn't panned out he'd moved on to the daughter of another moneyed man. But Jake Brockton didn't seem interested in her money or family connections. And she'd broken up with Hugh because there was zero chemistry between them and she didn't want to tie herself to a man she didn't feel any passion for, who simply wanted a suitable wife. But with Jake, her libido was jumping all over the place.

Sure, she didn't know everything about him, but that would change with time. And she wasn't about to start being paranoid, even if her sister believed she was crazy for trusting a man she hardly knew. Maddie had been pining for Zach for years before she summoned the courage to do something about it, and although Valene wanted to settle down and start nesting, she wanted to be in a relationship with someone who cared about her.

"Would you like to meet the man in my life?" she asked suddenly.

His blue eyes widened. "The what?"

Valene smiled. "My dog."

His mouth curled at the edges. "I'd like that very much."

She pushed the plate aside and quickly finished her drink. "Then let's go."

Jake was conscious of how quiet Valene was on the drive to her place. She lived on the ground floor, and as she opened the door to her condo, he heard the rattle of excited feet clamoring over floorboards.

The short but powerful-looking bulldog came rushing down the hall to greet her and turned around in frenzied circles at her feet, making guttural sounds low in his throat. He had an underbite and slobber oozing from one side of his mouth.

"Isn't he adorable?" she said and crouched down to pet the animal. "My beautiful boy."

Jake laughed. He had several working dogs on the ranch, but Sheba was his pet. She was dainty and fluffy and considered herself quite the princess. Quite the opposite of the very unattractive dog who suddenly registered Jake's presence and started barking like crazy. He woofed and growled and was clearly standing his ground and making it known who was the boss around the place.

"Beautiful?" he queried, ignoring the growling.

"He is to me," she said and stood. "Bruce, this is Jake and he's a friend of mine, and he's very nice and I like him a lot, so be a good boy and don't slobber over his jeans or chew his feet off, okay?"

The dog stopped barking, angled his head to the side and let out a loud woof before he briefly rubbed against Jake's ankles, sniffed his boots and, clearly making the decision that Jake was not a threat to his beloved owner, trotted off down the hallway.

"You passed the test." Valene grinned.

"There was a test?"

She laughed. "Well, of course. Bruce always gets to meet my friends."

Jake liked that she considered him a friend. However, he certainly didn't want to get stuck in that category. Not when he was so attracted to her. "Well, I'm glad he approves."

She laughed again and invited him to take a tour of the condo. It was large and spacious, with polished wood floors, two bedrooms and bathrooms, its own laundry facility, a huge French provincial–style kitchen, and spacious dining and living room areas. A wall of windows overlooked the yard, and yet the place was surprisingly private. Showcasing her good taste, the furnishings were quality and understated, and it occurred to him that they had that in common, too.

"Would you like coffee?"

Jake turned and discovered she was directly behind him. They were close, barely a foot apart, and the proximity sent his body into high-alert mode. She was looking up, her chin tilted at an alluring angle, her brown eyes warm and eminently welcoming. Jake reached out and touched her hair, threading the silky strands through his fingers.

"Valene," he said softly, the blood simmering in his veins. "Would it be okay if I kissed you now?"

Her eyes darkened, and after a moment she spoke. "Yes."

Jake curled one hand around her nape and drew her closer. Her mouth parted slightly, as though she was thinking, waiting, anticipating his kiss. He bent his head and looked directly into her eyes, feeling the connection between them down to the soles of his feet. He urged her a little closer and she pressed against him. His other arm moved around her and settled on her hip as he bent down and touched her mouth with his own. He gently anchored her head and slowly deepened the kiss. Her lips parted and she sighed against his mouth, driving away all coherent thought as she accepted his tongue into her mouth. The kiss was hot and intense and blisteringly arousing, but Jake wasn't about to ask for anything else. He just kissed her. He didn't move his hands to her rib cage like he longed to do, he didn't stroke the swell of her breasts, he didn't press closer to make his arousal more obvious. He simply enjoyed the taste and feel of her tongue dancing around with his for those few intoxicating moments.

In the end, it was Valene who pulled back, and Jake released her instantly. She took a step backward, her breath coming out sharply, her eyes darkened with a heady kind of desire that shook him to the very core.

And then she spoke.

"I'm not going to have sex with you today," she said quietly and crossed her arms. "If that's what you—"

"It's not," he assured her. "It was a kiss. I've told you that I'm not interested in rushing into this, Valene, and I mean it. I like you, and I'm clearly very attracted to you."

"Actually, up until about two minutes ago I was almost convinced you'd put me into the friend zone. I'm pleased to know you haven't."

He smiled, captivated by her honesty. "I thought the same about you."

She smiled. "I'm not used to being around a man who can show so much restraint."

Jake laughed. "Restraint? It's not that. The truth is, I don't want to screw things up with you. We hardly know each other and we need to spend a lot more time together. And frankly, you don't strike me as a casual-sex kind of woman."

"I'm not," she said flatly. "I've had two relationships and they were both disappointing. I've never had a one-night stand. I've never picked a guy up in a bar. I've never had sex outside of a serious relationship. I'm boring and straitlaced in that way. The most outrageous thing I've ever done in my romantic life is use that dating app."

"Ditto," he said quietly. "And, Valene, you are anything but boring. But I hear you. I've had three serious relationships and the last one ended really badly, so I'm cautious about getting caught up in something too quickly. I like you a lot," he admitted. "And I want to get to know you. I'd like to date you. And kiss you. And yeah," he said, pausing as he took a long breath, "at some point I would like to make love to you. But, for now, let's just get to know one another, okay?"

She looked instantly relieved. And then she regarded him thoughtfully. "Why was your last breakup so bad?"

"It just didn't work out," he replied quickly. "I think I told you how we knew one another in high school and a few years back we reconnected. But it was a mistake. We were too different."

Jake wasn't about to admit that he'd caught Patrice in bed with one of the contractors he'd hired to remodel the ranch house—a renovation she'd insisted on because the house, like him, wasn't good enough for her. Maybe one day he'd tell Valene the real story, but for now she didn't need to know the sordid details.

"I know what you mean," she said and then spent a moment telling him about her last boyfriend and how he was handpicked by her overprotective father. "I guess after the way things went with Diego, I can't blame Dad for smothering me a little."

The reminder that her ex-boyfriend had been after her family's money struck a guilty chord in Jake's gut. He hadn't told Valene the truth about himself because he didn't want his wealth to muddy the waters between them, when the truth was, she'd been on the receiving end of a gold-digging ex and would probably understand. But something held him back from admitting the truth. For one, he'd heard rumors that the Fortunado empire wasn't as rock solid as it had once been. According to his friends and business acquaintances and word on the street, there had been some shady things going on with everyone associated with the Fortune family—including Kenneth Fortunado.

"I thought you were making coffee," he said casually and walked toward the kitchen counter.

She looked relieved by the digression and quickly prepared two cups of coffee. "Cookie?" she asked and held out a small cookie jar.

"Did you bake them?"

She laughed. "Ha, are you serious? I can't cook. I suppose you can?"

Jake smiled. "A little. Enough to get by. Can I ask you a question?"

She nodded. "Sure."

"You're related to the Fortune family, correct?"

Her brows instantly came together. "Yes."

"But you don't talk about it?"

She shrugged. "No," she replied, handing him his coffee. "My dad prefers not to talk about it," she said after a moment. "So, we don't."

"Is there bad blood?"

She let out a sigh and came around the counter, perching herself on the edge of a stool. "More like no blood. My dad didn't know about his family tree until recently. He found out he was Julius Fortune's son and had a few other illegitimate half brothers. It's been kind of messy ever since. My grandmother chose the name Fortunado as a way of enabling my dad to have a link with his family, but he doesn't have any interest in being a part of them."

"Do you?" Jake asked and sipped his coffee.

"I'm not sure," she replied. "I mean, I am *intrigued*, of course. How could I not be? It's the Fortunes. They're legendary in this state, for one reason or another. Plus, my father and Gerald Robinson of Robinson Tech are half brothers, since Gerald Robinson is really Jerome Fortune and Julius's son. The last year has been full of surprises, to say the least. And one of Gerald's daughters is married to a Mendoza and my sister Schuyler is also married to a Mendoza…so the huge disconnect between the families is not as wide as it used to be. It's been difficult for everyone. Particularly since so many strange things have happened."

Jake met her gaze. "What kind of strange things?"

"Robinson Tech was hacked. We've been losing clients at both the Austin and Houston offices, which almost seems less like coincidence and more like sabotage according to my sister and her husband, Zach. And there was a terrible fire at the Robinson estate."

"I heard about that," Jake said. "Makes me kind of pleased that you don't have anything to do with them."

"It's complicated," she said quietly. "I have a crazy family tree."

"Not me," he admitted. "Dull as dishwater. Mom and Dad loved each other. No family skeletons. We're boring and uneventful."

"I envy you," she said on a sigh. "In my family, every day is potentially a disaster waiting to happen. And it doesn't help that my dad won't talk about it, not even to Mom. He used to talk to my grandmother, I guess, but I think he's just over the whole Fortune thing. It's probably why he vacations so much now. I mean, he and Mom did plan on doing a lot of trips once he retired, so they haven't spent much time at home lately. They came back for Maddie's wedding and then took off again."

"You miss them?" Jake suggested.

She nodded, suddenly looking incredibly young. "I do," she admitted. "I guess I'm one of those crazy people who actually like their parents."

"You're not crazy," Jake assured her. "I like my parents, too. In fact, my mother is going to want to meet you at some point in the near future. She thinks I've been in a much better mood this week."

Valene laughed loudly. "I think I like your mom already."

"And of course Cassidy is taking all the credit." He grinned. "My sister is quite the matchmaker."

"Well, you can tell her she does good work," she said quietly. "Speaking of which, I really need to get some work done this afternoon, or Maddie is going to fire me."

Jake didn't believe her. "Of course she won't do that."

"She might." Valene shrugged. "I've lost two listings in the past week, and the company lost several more in the last month. No listing, no sales…it's a vicious circle."

Jake experienced an acute sense of concern. "Do you know why?"

"No," she replied. "I think I've lost my mojo."

"I'm sure you'll get it back."

"I hope so," she said. "I need to get a few more exclusive clients to prove myself. Which means I have to start pounding the pavement this week." She took a sip of her coffee, then looked up at him. "Um, there's a charity thing I have to go to on Friday night. My sister Maddie and her husband will be there. It's at one of the hotels in town, a fund-raiser for the Fortunado Foundation. Would you like to accompany me?"

Jake's gaze narrowed. "As your date?"

She nodded fractionally. "Do you have a suit?"

Jake heard the uncertainty in her voice, and for some reason it irked him. "Yes, I do."

She looked relieved. "So…you'll go?"

"Sure."

"Great. You can meet me here and we'll go in my car."

Her car? He didn't need her to spell out what that meant, since she'd only seen him driving the old Ranger. Jake drained the coffee cup and got to his feet. "I should bail and let you get some work done."

She slid off the stool. "Thank you for a lovely day."

"Anytime."

She stood on her toes and kissed his cheek and then again, a little closer to his mouth. Jake grasped her shoulders and kissed her gently on the lips. She sighed against him, and it made him smile. He lingered for a few seconds, kissing her again, inhaling the scent of her hair and her lovely skin, tasting the sweetness of her mouth.

And as he left her condo and walked back toward his truck and then drove off, Jake realized one thing. He liked Valene. A lot. Which meant he had to come clean about his past and his present. And soon.

Chapter Six

"You went where?"

Valene was standing by the water cooler in the lunch room on Monday morning, talking to Maddie and getting the third degree about her date with Jake. "An animal shelter."

She saw Maddie's frown. "Why?"

"He volunteers there. He has since he was a teenager. He's really perfect."

Maddie didn't look convinced. "Did you sleep with him last night?"

Valene no doubt looked as affronted as she felt. "Of course not. I'm not like that. And neither is Jake, which you'd know if you would stop being all judgmental about him not being wealthy or successful. Frankly, Maddie, I didn't realize you were so bigoted."

Maddie didn't bother to disguise her displeasure. "You can be as smart with me as you want, but I can see you're really falling for this guy, and I'm concerned. I'm certainly not judging him. I'm sure he's very nice and really charming, but you can't make a silk purse out of a sow's ear, Val. And I know you're all starry-eyed because he's attractive and something of a novelty, and he's taking you to see puppies and kittens and bringing you your favorite coffee, but do you honestly think he'll fit into your real world? I mean, long-term?"

Truthfully, Valene had no idea. She liked Jake. A lot. She was more attracted to him than she'd ever been to anyone, and his kisses were out of this world. But Maddie had a point. For starters, his lifestyle was the polar opposite of her own. And yet, she didn't care. A warning voice in the back of her mind told her she was heading for heartbreak by falling for a penniless cowboy like Jake—but he made her feel so good about herself. So in tune with herself. And Valene had never experienced that before.

"I don't know," she said to her sister with a sigh. "But I know he's the first man I've ever met who makes me feel as though he likes me for me, and who is completely and utterly himself. He's not trying to be someone or something he isn't, and he certainly isn't trying to impress me with some ulterior motive. He's probably the most honorable and self-sufficient man I have ever met. He's honest, Maddie, and with my history, that's something I'm looking for. Please try to understand that I just want to see where this goes."

"I do understand, Val, and I truly want you to be happy. But please go slowly."

"I will," she said. "I promise. As long as you promise to let me live my own life and not judge Jake too quickly or harshly."

"I promise," she assured her.

"You can prove it on Friday night," Valene said and smiled. "I invited him to be my date to the charity dinner."

Maddie looked dubious, then sighed. "Okay. Now, I had better get back to work. I'm leaving for Austin around lunchtime and will be back Wednesday afternoon. Zach's staying here to connect with a couple of important clients."

"I need to get back to work, too," Val said, grinning. "Or my boss will send me packing."

"No, she won't. You're far too valuable around here."

"Even though I'm losing clients left, right and center?"

"Even then," Maddie said and gave her a quick hug. "And we're all in this together, remember? You're not the only agent who's lost clients. It's happening to us all. See you soon."

The following days were busy for Valene. And surprising. Because on Tuesday morning she received a call from a man who introduced himself as Karl Messer. He was a property developer and his company, the Messer Group, was building one of the new high-rises on the east side of the city, one that was zoned both residential and commercial, and he wanted to meet with her the following day to discuss listing the place exclusively with Fortunado Real Estate. When she ended the call, Valene's hands were shaking. It would be an amazing coup to land an exclusive listing with one of the hottest property developers in Houston. Usually Zach handled the larger accounts, and since Maddie had insisted she run everything by her brother-in-law, Valene tapped on his office door later that day.

"Would you like me to come to the meeting with you?" he asked once she'd told him the details.

Valene bit her lip. "I'd like to have the opportunity to land the deal myself. Is that okay?"

Zach, who was undoubtedly one of the greatest guys she had ever known, nodded. "Of course. You know I'm here to support you."

"Thank you, Zach. I won't let you down."

"I know that, Val. And remember that Maddie and I are one hundred percent behind you."

That thought stayed with her when she met with Karl Messer the following day. The meeting took place at the office on the construction site, and she was instantly impressed. Messer, in his early thirties, clearly was in command of the business he had inherited from his uncle a few years earlier. He was tall and attractive and acted completely professional toward her. The meeting ran for over an hour, and then he gave her a brief tour of the construction site. She ended the meeting with his assurance that he was committed to working with Fortunado Real Estate and would give her exclusivity on both the residential and commercial properties.

When Valene returned to her office, it was after four and she was humming and about to drop off her bag before she headed to see Zach when she noticed a cylindrical package on her desk. She recognized the name of the courier company and assumed it was something work related. But when she opened the package, she discovered a scrolled paper inside. She rolled it out and laughed delightedly. It was a sketch, intricately done, of a bulldog. Her bulldog, it seemed, one poking tooth and drool included. And written at the bottom in a dark and cursive scrawl were a few words.

From the other man in your life...

She knew instantly that it was from Jake. So, her sexy cowboy was talented as well as gorgeous. Valene remembered him telling her over dinner that he had liked to draw in high school, after he'd teased her about being on the math squad and the calculus team.

She grabbed her cell and sent him a text.

I love it. Bruce looks adorable. Thank you! V.

She waited a few minutes and then read the reply message.

My pleasure. Looking forward to seeing you again. J.

Valene's entire body thrummed. She texted back immediately.

If you want to call me tonight, that would be okay. V.

It took about two seconds to get a reply.

It's a date. Eight o'clock. J.

"Why do you look so happy?"

She turned to see both her sister and brother-in-law standing in the doorway. Valene rolled up the scroll and smiled. "I had a good meeting," she said, deciding not to show them the picture Jake had sent her, because it felt personal and ridiculously intimate and she didn't want to share her enjoyment with anyone.

She spent the next five minutes outlining every detail of the meeting she had with Karl Messer and how he'd promised her exclusivity and, if the arrangement was successful, the same entitlement for his next highrise project, as well. It was the biggest deal she had ever brokered, and she knew both Maddie and Zach would be proud of her. And they were.

"How did you meet Mr. Messer?" her sister asked.

Valene shrugged. "He called me. He said he'd heard good things about Fortunado."

Maddie nodded. "He's got a good reputation as a builder. Good safety record. I think Gavin knows him," she said of their recently engaged lawyer brother. "I'll ask for a rundown next time I talk to him."

"I wonder if Gavin recommended us?" Val mused. "Well, if he did, Mr. Messer didn't mention it. And it appears to be a genuine offer, so I'll have the contracts started tomorrow."

Both Maddie and Zach nodded. "Good work," Maddie said and smiled. "It will help ease the sting when I tell you that we lost the McGovern place this afternoon."

Valene's stomach sank. "That's not possible. Just last week I took—"

"It's possible," Zach said gently. "I spoke to the owner myself."

"Was it something I did?" she asked.

"No," Zach promised her. "Just business. Don't take this personally, Val."

But she did. Because it felt personal. It felt as though her career was slipping from her fingertips. Sure, the Messer deal was huge, but she'd worked hard to cultivate the other clients and couldn't believe so many were dropping off the Fortunado books. Not only her clients, but two of the other agents in the office had lost clients in the last month.

Which was what she told Jake when she spoke to him later that night. He'd called at exactly eight o'clock and Valene was eagerly waiting for his call, keen to hear his voice and listen to his words of encouragement and steady reasoning. Which she did. He was exactly the tonic she needed.

"I'm sure you'll work this out," he said assuredly. "Every business goes through tough times, Valene."

"I know," she sighed. "I just hate letting people down."

"Didn't you say both your sister and brother-in-law told you not to take it to heart?"

"Yes," she replied. "But I always do. I always have. And I know Maddie is worried. With Dad retired and out of town, it just feels like we're under attack. I know that sounds dramatic, and I know I probably sound like a spoiled little girl whose daddy isn't around to pick up the pieces of the disaster she's gotten herself into, but I can't help how I feel."

"You're not a little girl and you're not spoiled," Jake said evenly. "You're an accomplished young woman with a great career. Did you know that your name means strong?"

She chuckled softly. "Yes, I know. Did you look that up?"

"I was curious," he replied. "It also means you are dynamic and visionary. Use that part of yourself to your advantage. Like you did today with the new client you got."

"I'm not sure I did much," she said honestly. "He came to me. I didn't have to pound the pavement to find him."

"Sometimes it's not how you get opportunity that makes you successful. It's what you do with it."

She took a breath and felt the air fill her lungs, calming her immediately. "Thank you. I always feel better when I talk to you."

He was silent, and she wondered if she'd gone too far,

said too much, made him feel uncomfortable by intimating that there was more going on between them than there actually was. But oddly, it didn't feel as though they had only known one another a week. It felt as though they had been friends for a long time.

"Valentine's Day is a little over a week away," he reminded her. "Save the date, okay? I'd like to spend the day with you."

Valene's heart skipped a beat. Never in her wildest dreams had she imagined she'd have a date for Valentine's Day. "I'd love to spend the day with you. So, I'll see you Friday night for the dinner."

"For sure. Sweet dreams, Valene."

She ended the call and spent the next hour or so thinking about him. For a man who made his living on the land, he was surprisingly insightful and philosophical.

She dreamed about him that night, imagining his kiss and his touch, and when she awoke she was unusually fatigued. He texted her around nine to wish her a nice day, and it put her in a good mood all morning. Her day brightened around lunchtime when she took a call from another prospective client, a rancher about half an hour out of town who owned a few hundred acres he wanted to sell. He was a gruff kind of man who got straight to the point and said he wouldn't be messing around with other agents as long as he had her word that she would give him one hundred percent loyalty. Valene liked him immediately and made arrangements to visit his place the following Monday.

She spoke to her mother that afternoon, staying mute about the troubles the business was having, figuring it was Maddie and Zach's place to talk to their father about it. Instead, she mentioned that she'd met someone and brushed over the details, just focusing on how nice he was and how much she liked him and how she looked forward to them meeting him when they returned from their vacation.

On Friday afternoon she left work early and headed for the salon, getting her hair and makeup done. She'd bought a new gown for the event, a red halter that showed off way too much skin, so she paired it with a black organza wrap and matching shoes. The color was about as wild as she got and she twirled in front of the mirror a few times, under Bruce's strict scrutiny, and then decided she looked nice enough. She slipped on her coat, grabbed her bag and headed outside, waiting for Jake by the front gate.

He arrived exactly on time, pulling up in a huge, hulking and very new cherry-red SUV. It looked like they weren't taking her Lexus, after all.

When he got out of the vehicle, he looked so hot she almost fainted. He wore a black suit, white shirt, shiny black boots and a bolo tie. He was just about the most gorgeous man she had ever seen. Clean shaven, his jaw was smooth, and she itched with the need to feel his mouth pressed against hers. He kissed her cheek and opened the passenger door.

"Nice rig," she said and hauled herself up. When he came around to the driver's side and got in, she asked, "Borrowed?"

"It belongs on the ranch."

She nodded. "Well, it's good you can borrow it for special occasions. Hey, I got another prospective client yesterday—someone who owns a ranch out near Fulshear. That's your territory, isn't it?"

"Close enough," he replied as he pulled onto the road. "So, where are we going?"

She gave him the directions and they headed off.

The hotel was one of the best in town, and she knew the ballroom would be transformed for the event. A jazz band was expected to perform, along with several well-known entertainers. The tables seated ten and had cost a fortune, so the attendees would be a who's who of Houston society. The funds raised would go directly to the Fortunado Foundation and then be funneled out to several other charities that helped women and children.

Jake helped her from the SUV, dropped the keys into the valet's hand and then led her into the hotel.

She checked in her coat and heard Jake's breath suck in as he stared at her, wide-eyed.

"You look incredible."

"Thank you," she said and placed her hand on his lapel. "You look sharp yourself. Thank you for dressing up. I know you're probably more comfortable in jeans and a Stetson. In fact, I prefer jeans and a T-shirt myself most of the time, but every now and then I have to dress up for one of Mom's galas."

His gaze lingered on her bare shoulders. "I'm starting to like your mom more and more."

Valene grinned. "She's disappointed she couldn't be here tonight, but the dates conflicted with the vacation she and Dad had planned. I'm sure Maddie will be in charge in her usual way. Actually, I think Zach is doing the honors as MC."

He nodded. "So, jazz?" he queried close to her ear as they entered the ballroom and made their way to their table. "Is this payback for the cowboy dancing?"

Valene chuckled. Gosh, he was sexy. The feel of his breath so close to her skin heated her blood, and she swayed toward him. The place was buzzing with people and she noticed that their table was already filling with couples. Jake pulled out her seat politely, and as she sat down it occurred to her that he was incredibly well mannered.

Before she had a chance to look around the table, he introduced himself, and Valene recognized two of the other couples sitting there. They were business associates of Zach's, nice enough people, but rich and often acting just a little too entitled for her taste. Perhaps that's why Val didn't have a lot of friends in her circle. She had two close friends from college who still regularly kept in contact with her, and her friend Adele, but most of her socializing was done with her work colleagues or her sisters when they were in town. Friday nights were often download time at the Thirsty Ox, an English-style pub just down the street from the office, but Val hadn't been for a few weeks. And since meeting Jake, most of her spare time had been filled with seeing him or thinking about him.

For a moment she worried he might be out of his depth with their tablemates. But no, he was clearly at ease and making conversation. Then she felt small-minded for thinking such a thing. Jake Brockton was no small-town hick. Lack of college education aside, he was smart and articulate and obviously at home in any scenario. She was about to join the conversation when her sister and brother-in-law appeared.

Jake was on his feet in a microsecond and took Maddie's hand, then he shook Zach's. Val quickly noticed Maddie's surprise and the gathering approval once her sister looked him over. Val felt vindicated, and also a little resentful. She hadn't brought Jake to the gala so he could be on show: she'd brought him because she wanted to be with him. Her sister's reaction simply proved what Val had suspected, that everyone stood in judgment.

And she realized that she'd been like that herself. Asking him to wear a suit. Suggesting they arrive in her car. Intimating that he had to be someone other than who he was to be acceptable company. Everything about those comments screamed entitled, spoiled, snobby, and she was deeply ashamed of herself.

"Are you okay, Valene?"

Jake's voice, close and whisper soft, brought her out of her thoughts. He was back in his seat and regarding her with concern.

"I'm fine," she assured him quietly, discreetly touching his arm. "I just wanted to say I'm glad you're here with me tonight and I like you…just as you are. I like your integrity and your honesty."

His gaze narrowed. "Valene…we need to talk about some things."

"What things?"

He was about to reply when the band played an introduction number, indicating the show was about to commence. "Later," he said and leaned in to kiss her cheek. "Nothing will change between us, I promise."

Oddly, she was put instantly at ease. Because Jake could do that. His deep voice and quiet confidence made her believe that anything was possible…including a real future with him…a man she was falling for. Big time.

Jake shifted in his seat as Valene's brother-in-law took to the stage. He'd never met the man before tonight, but he was well acquainted with several other people he'd spotted in the room. The irony of the situation was not lost on him. Last year he'd bought a table for the event for several of his customers. He hadn't attended himself, since he was neck-deep in divorcing Patrice at the time, but he felt foolish for not remembering why the Fortunado name was so familiar to him when he'd first met Valene.

He listened to the MC, conscious that Valene's fingers were resting on his arm, curling around his bicep. After the first speech, a comedian took to the stage, a well-known performer who cleverly dissed politics and social media and several self-obsessed celebrities. Beside him, Valene's soft laughter filled his chest with a heady kind of happiness. He enjoyed her company a lot. Too much, probably. And they were getting closer every time they were together. Becoming lovers was inevitable and he didn't want there to be any secrets between them, but... A warning voice lingered in his head. Something wasn't right with the Fortunado family. Something he suspected had everything to do with their link to the Fortunes and Robinsons. He wasn't sure why he felt there was a connection—instinct perhaps, or the street smarts he'd picked up over the years. They rarely failed him.

The band started shortly afterward, and they were entertained by a jazz singer. Sure, jazz wasn't his thing, but Jake could appreciate talent. As he listened, he thought of Valene's sister. Maddie had spoken to him a little, her curious expression making it plain that she was keeping a watchful eye on her little sister. She was a very beautiful woman and was clearly besotted with her husband and business partner. Jake admired the way they had made both their personal and professional relationships work. In a way, he envied them, since it looked so easy. But he knew from experience that it wasn't. Patrice had done a great job at convincing him that marriage was hard work. Still, he had good memories of his parents' marriage, and Valene often talked about how much in love her mother and father still were. And he was pleased that Valene was well loved and that her family was watching out for her.

Family was everything to Jake.

Which was why he'd been happy when Patrice had told him she was pregnant. They were already separated, already in the throes of divorce, but he'd believed her when she'd said the baby was his. Looking back, Jake couldn't believe he'd been so foolishly naive. He'd offered to raise the child with a shared custody arrangement, or alone if that's what she preferred. But that wasn't Patrice's endgame. Her motive was the same as it had always been—to grab as much of his money as she could. It was only when he said he wasn't about to pay for the privilege of being a parent that she admitted the child wasn't his.

The announcement had hurt more than he'd believed possible. And it turned his heart to stone for a while. Or at the very least, made him overcautious of getting involved with anyone.

Until Valene.

Of course, the warning bells were pealing like crazy.

The possibility of marriage and kids was way off into the future, but being around Valene gave him hope that he could open himself up again to feel something for someone. And it wasn't simply desire. Of course, he wanted her. She was beautiful and sexy and drove him crazy, but there was more to her than a pretty face, seductive brown eyes and incredible curves. Valene had gumption and intelligence and wit. She was the whole package. There didn't seem to be anything narcissistic or covetous about her. Sure, she was young and inexperienced and a little spoiled, but she carried herself like a woman who knew exactly who and what she was, even if she sometimes didn't believe it.

Then why can't I tell her the truth?

Jake knew why.

Fear.

If she knew who he really was, what he'd made of himself, how could he be certain that her feelings for him were real? Were pure? Were what he needed to get the taste of bitterness and betrayal from his mouth? She liked him. She'd said it several times, and he was savvy enough to see the desire and genuine attraction in her eyes. But since both her sisters had recently found partners, how could Jake be sure she wasn't simply in love with the idea of being in love? He couldn't. Only time would tell if their budding relationship would go the distance. And with time came the very real chance that she would discover who and what he was before he took the opportunity to tell her himself. She believed he was a simple ranch hand and in a way that was true. Jake still worked the ranch as he had done since before he'd bought the place. But she had him pegged as a ranch hand who lived week to week, who owned a beat-up truck and who could afford jeans, not jewels. Someone she had to ask to wear a suit to a fancy shindig like a gala dinner. Someone who couldn't get a reservation at one of the busiest restaurants in town. Someone without influence.

When the truth was quite the opposite.

He was a successful ranch owner who had a considerable portfolio of other properties and investments in several developments around town—including one with Karl Messer. They'd been friends since high school and were now connected through business, even though Jake insisted on being a silent partner in any venture he invested in. And Karl was discreet, which was why he'd set him up with Valene. He'd wanted to help her, to let her shimmer the way she was destined to shine. He wasn't sure she'd be entirely pleased that he'd interfered, however, so staying quiet about his involvement was probably the best option at the moment.

"Would you like to dance, cowboy?"

Valene's soft and seductive voice whispered close to his ear. He noticed there were several couples on the dance floor. "Love to."

He took her hand and got to his feet, and within seconds they were on the dance floor.

"You know," she said as she swayed, resting a hand on his shoulder while the other was enclosed firmly within his, "this isn't so different from dancing cowboy style."

Jake urged her a little closer. "Not so different at all."

Someone he knew was dancing nearby and recognized him, and Jake responded with a brief nod. The last thing he wanted was to be outed on the dance floor. He pressed his face against her hair, inhaling the intoxicating scent. And he was a goner. He was so into Valene he couldn't think straight. Even the guys who worked for him had mentioned he was distracted. He was thinking about Valene when he should have been doing a dozen other things. He was dreaming about Valene. He was fantasizing about her.

He was, Jake realized foolishly, half in love with a woman he'd known a little over a week.

Chapter Seven

Valene lost sight of Jake in the room and scanned the crowd. They'd parted company for a while when Maddie had insisted she help meet and greet the band and guest artists who had all donated their time for the charity event. It took about ten seconds to find him, though, near the bar area, talking to three other men of various ages. The oldest of the group said something and the rest of them laughed, Jake included, and then one of them slapped him on the back as though they had been acquainted for years. It struck her as odd behavior, as she was sure he didn't know anyone in the room besides her.

She made a direct line to him through the crowd when he looked her way, as though they were connected by some invisible radar. He quickly excused himself and met her halfway across the room.

"Having a good time?" she asked when he took her hand and raised it to his mouth.

"Of course. You?"

Valene's brows rose high at his benign reply. "My sister thinks you're ridiculously good-looking."

He laughed softly. "And what do you think?"

"I think you were making friends over there," she remarked. "*And* I think you are perfectly at ease in a room full of people."

"People are just people, Valene. There's no mystery to making conversation."

"I'm not so sure," she said and allowed him to lead her away from the crowd and back to their now vacant table. "I've always been considered something of a party girl, but the truth is, I've never been that great in crowds. I think I'm really more of an introvert, despite my reputation."

He chuckled and kissed her cheek, lingering around the soft skin beneath her lobe. The sensation turned her bones to liquid and she sighed, curling her fingers around his arm. In all her life, Val had never had such an intense physical reaction to anyone.

"I think," he whispered against her skin, "that you are perfect, Ms. Fortunado."

Val pulled back a fraction and met his gaze, conscious that to anyone watching, they would appear like lovers who had known one another intimately. There was an intensity about the connection they shared that defied logic, considering the short time they had known one another. She'd heard about it, of course, about instant attraction, the lightning-bolt kind. Even her sister Schuyler had declared that she believed in lust at first sight since she'd met Carlo. But as attracted as she was to Jake, there was also something else going on. Something deeper than pure sexual attraction. She enjoyed his company, experienced pleasure when he spoke or laughed, found herself thinking of him every day.

It's like at first sight.

Who am I kidding?

Valene wasn't an expert at deep emotion, but she'd witnessed real love firsthand by watching her parents' happy and successful marriage. It was something she wanted to emulate, like Maddie and Schuyler had recently done. It was important to her that she spend her life with one man, someone she could have children with, walk alongside through the challenges of life.

Someone like Jake.

He was strong and sincere and clearly valued honesty and integrity. She liked that about him. She knew it was what she was looking for.

"I've never met a man like you," she said softly.

Jake touched her cheek. "Like what?"

"So…together. So…real."

He chuckled. "I've been called a lot of things, but never that."

"Who were you talking to back there?" she asked.

He shrugged. "Just someone I know from the ranch. So, would you like to dance some more?"

"Sure."

They spent the next half hour on the dance floor, and she spotted Maddie and Zach swaying to a romantic number, engrossed in each other and clearly in love. And surprisingly, the spike of envy she expected didn't come, because somehow, she was in the middle of her own romantic fairy tale. Valene pressed herself into Jake's embrace, inhaling the sexy, woodsy scent of his cologne, feeling his strong chest beneath her cheek. She noticed a few things about him as they danced close together, like the fact that his cuff links were stamped with his initials, and his tie bar was made of solid silver. It seemed at odds, somehow, with his workingman, ranch hand image.

"I like your cuff links," she said and touched the ornate bar with her finger.

"They were my grandfather's," he supplied. "I was named after him."

Val nodded. "You have a strong sense of family."

He pressed a hand into the small of her back. "Family is everything."

"I agree," she said and swayed against him, loving the feel of his hand on her, even through her gown, and the heat it created on her skin. "I love my family very much. And I really want to have a family of my own one day. You said you wanted kids, right?"

"Yes."

It was a simple response. Too simple. Because Valene picked up on something hollow about the way he said it, as though he was suddenly filled with memory, and sadness.

"Jake…is everything okay?"

"Fine."

"If you've had enough, we can leave."

He shook his head. "And miss out on dancing this close with you?" he replied. "Not a chance."

Val felt light-headed, and for a second she wondered if women still swooned, because being around Jake made her feel all kinds of things she wasn't sure existed.

They danced for a while longer, and then once they returned to the table, she told him she was ready to go. Val found her sister, congratulated her and Zach on a fabulous event, and said she'd see them both the following week.

"Why don't you stop by the house tomorrow night

and bring Jake?" her sister suggested. "I'll cook. Or Zach will cook." Maddie grinned. "Or we'll order take-out."

An evening under the microscope with her very opinionated and judgmental sister? Val was about to refuse the invitation when she saw Jake nod slightly and relax. "Ah...okay. I'll bring dessert."

"No need," Maddie said and waved a hand. "I have it covered."

They were driving back to her apartment about ten minutes later when she spoke about her sister's offer. "We don't have to go if you don't want to."

Jake glanced her way for a second. "I'm happy to do whatever makes *you* happy, Valene. You've said many times that family is important to you. And your sister and her husband are nice people."

"She'll give you the third degree," Val said and made a face. "Are you up for that?"

Jake chuckled. "I'll cope. If Cassidy brought home someone I didn't know, I'd do the same thing."

"She's so lucky to have you."

"Likewise for your siblings," he said quietly. "Maddie is only watching out for you. Don't get frustrated because she loves you so much."

Val sighed and relaxed in the seat. "You make everything seem easier."

"Family isn't easy. But they're who we have, so there's no point fighting it. I'm sure there are days when Cassidy feels as though she's smothered and overprotected and that's why she went away to college. It's instinct, I guess, to want to protect the people we love."

He had a point. For most of her life, Val had been overprotected by her parents and siblings. She hadn't balked against it, hadn't overreacted, but sometimes

her resentment had simmered along the surface, looking for an escape route. She'd never acted out, never
done anything wild or outrageous, but she'd also never
complained about the attention, either.

"If I told my parents they smothered me, they'd be
so hurt."

"Then don't," Jake replied as they drove through the
city. "You can be independent without being alone."

She sighed. "I live in a condo my father bought. I
work in a place run by my sister. That doesn't sound
like the life of an independent person, does it?"

"We can all look for ways to devalue the meaning
of our life," he remarked quietly. "I guess it's how we
manage our good fortune that matters the most."

"Like my mom does," she remarked. "Working with
the Fortunado Foundation. Or you do at the shelter."
She let out a long breath. "Do you know, the last pair of
jeans I bought cost nearly four hundred dollars? Imagine how many rescue animals that money could feed at
the shelter. Or how many people it could help through
the Fortunado Foundation. Gah… I'm a spoiled child."

Jake chuckled softly and grabbed her hand, holding
it firmly within his. "You're incredible, Valene. You're
passionate and funny, and the world needs that kind
of passion."

She looked down at their linked hands. "Do you?"

"That's a loaded question."

She laughed. "I really like being with you. And flirting with you," she added.

"I've noticed."

A few minutes later he parked outside her condo and
quickly came around to the passenger side, where he
held her door for her.

"Do you want to come inside?" she asked.

"Yes," he replied and gathered her into his strong arms. "Which is why I'm going to kiss you good-night and then leave."

Val experienced a mix of disappointment and appreciation. He was right. It was still too soon for her to have sex with him. Even though she wanted it more and more every time they were together. But she appreciated the fact that he knew it.

He kissed her, slowly and deeply, and by the time he raised his head she was clinging to him, desperate for more of his mouth on hers. She touched his face, felt how his skin was cool from the night air and was instantly caught up in his glittering gaze.

"Good night, Jake."

He made arrangements to pick her up the following evening, kissed her again before wishing her sweet dreams and then waited until she was safely inside before leaving.

She sent him a text about an hour later, when she knew he would be home and not driving.

I had a lovely time tonight. Thank you. Part of me wishes you'd stayed. V.

A message came back within seconds.

Ditto. Stop text torturing me. Good night, sweetheart. J.

Val was still smiling, still ridiculously happy when she awoke the next morning. She went in to work for a couple of hours to facilitate the Messer listing and took a call from Schuyler around eleven. They chatted for a while, mostly about Jake, and Schuyler squealed in delight that Val was so happy. Later, she made plans to meet with a couple of clients in Austin the following week and locked in several appointments.

She dropped by the supermarket after work to load up the rear of her Lexus with dog and cat food and then headed for the animal shelter, specifically to see Florence and drop off the donation, but also to spend a few minutes petting Digby, who'd become something of a favorite of hers. When she returned home she took Bruce for a walk, did some laundry, spent an idle half hour on Instagram and then went to the gym at the complex. By six she was showered and dressed and waiting for Jake.

He picked her up on time as always, in his old truck, and kissed her softly, and they headed for her sister's place. Maddie, of course, was her usual reserved and cautious self, but Zach was entertaining and a great host. Jake had stopped off to buy imported beer and wine, and soon after arriving they were all settled in the huge dining room. Maddie had gone all out ordering takeout, offering appetizers first and then a main meal that was delicious and loaded with carbs.

"Toscano's," Maddie announced when Jake complimented the porcini pasta dish. "It really is the best Italian place in the city, in my opinion. They do the most amazing beef ravioli."

Val glanced toward Jake and smiled. He hadn't flinched, hadn't moved a muscle, and Val was certain she had never met a more self-assured, quietly confident man in her life.

"You should take the Messer Group people there," Maddie told her. "A good meal is always a great way to break the ice with a new client. Probably best to try for lunch, though. It's impossible to get a dinner reservation. The place is always booked weeks ahead."

Val's mouth curled at the edges and when her gaze

met Jake's again, she saw the humor in his expression. She wasn't about to brag and say that her new boyfriend had only had to make a phone call to score them the best table in the place at a day's notice.

New boyfriend?

Is that what he is?

Val had been desperate not to label what they had, but they were into the second week of their acquaintance and it certainly felt like more than something casual. It felt real. Perhaps the most real relationship she had ever had.

Equally surprisingly, the evening at her sister's was pleasant. Maddie and Zach were perfect hosts, the food was wonderful and the conversation easy. Till Maddie brought up Jake's lack of a college education.

"Val said you left college in your first year?"

He nodded, unflinching. "That's right."

"What were you studying?"

"Art."

Valene wasn't surprised, considering the quality of the adorable portrait of Bruce he'd drawn freehand. But she was stunned that she hadn't asked him that question herself. They did, she realized, spend a lot more time talking about her than they did about his life or his past. It was something she intended to remedy. She certainly didn't want her sister learning things about him before she did.

"Why did you leave school?" Maddie asked, relentless.

"My father passed away and I was needed at home."

"That must have been a difficult decision."

"Not really," he replied. "My family needed me. And at the end of the day, family is all that matters. But of course, you know that."

It was the perfect shutdown. Val noticed the edge of "mind your own business" in his tone, but he was too polite to say it outright. And Maddie didn't know him well enough to pick up on anything other than his calm and quiet courtesy. They stayed another couple of hours, talking over dessert, which Jake declined, and then playing a few rounds of pool, two of which Jake won, much to Zach's good-humored irritation. As soon as they were in his truck and heading back to her condo, Val apologized.

"I'm so sorry about Maddie. She can be a pain in the neck about some things."

He chuckled. "You worry too much. She wasn't so bad."

Val sighed. "That's generous."

"She was right about one thing," Jake said and took a left onto the highway. "The beef ravioli at Toscano's is the best around."

Val laughed so loudly she snorted, which made Jake laugh. It was such a wonderful moment, and her heart fluttered madly. The more time she spent with Jake, the more she wanted to spend with him.

When they pulled up at her building, he was out of the vehicle and around to her side in seconds.

"So," she said, "are you coming in?"

Jake gently hauled her into his arms and kissed her soundly. "You know, Valene, I've never been the self-sacrificing type, so you better stop asking me that question."

She groaned and pressed against him, snaking her arms around his waist. "I'm sorry I didn't know about what you were studying in college. I should have known," she said and rested her ear against his heart. "I should have realized after that wonderful portrait you did of Bruce."

"Stop apologizing," he said softly. "And you better get inside, because it's getting colder out here, and I don't want either of us to catch pneumonia."

He left as soon as she was inside, and Val was uncharacteristically unhappy afterward, moping around her place for an hour or so before she showered and headed to bed, with Bruce firmly taking up his spot on one side.

"You better get used to the floor, buddy," she said playfully and petted him. "I'm pretty sure that spot is going to be taken up soon."

And as she drifted off to sleep, her thoughts and dreams were filled with images of the man who had captured her heart.

Val headed to Austin early on Tuesday morning and worked through until Wednesday afternoon and was back in Houston by six in the evening. On Thursday morning she headed out to Fulshear to meet with the owner whose listing she'd acquired the week before. It had been an eventful couple of days in Austin, and now she was back home she needed to focus on the week ahead. The Messer building was now hers to sell exclusively, and she had scored another prospective new client, a woman who owned a large estate in River Oaks and who had been recommended to her by Karl Messer. For her, things were definitely looking up, but the agency had lost another two clients and Zach was now talking conspiracy and sabotage. After what had happened to the Robinsons, and what were clearly more than coincidental losses at Fortunado Real Estate, everyone was taking the possibility of it being a real threat very seriously.

The upside was that she talked to Jake every night. He called her at eight o'clock in the evenings and they chatted for close to half an hour, discussing their days and anything else that came to mind. It was a lovely way to finish off the day, and she looked forward to hearing his voice each night more than she'd believed possible.

The land in Fulshear was cleared and fenced and had a small, neat dwelling and several water holes—it would be perfect for running stock. Val spent half an hour with the owner, Otis McAvoy, an ornery man in his midsixties who clearly had no tolerance for fools. But Val didn't mind straight talk and quite liked him. He would be a no-nonsense, no-fuss client who only wanted the best and fairest price for his land.

It was simple providence that made her drive past the Double Rock Ranch. Her GPS had diverted her down a shortcut and she spotted the ranch where Jake worked and lived. There was a huge picture of a dark stud bull on a sign beside the gate, along with the letters *JJB* and a phone number beneath.

She drove through the gates and up a long driveway, which was blanketed by lush coastal grasses, and pasture, which was dotted with mature oak and pecan trees. It was a postcard-perfect scene. As she drove farther she spotted a ranch house at the end of the driveway. The home was clearly in the midst of a renovation, as it was surrounded by scaffolding and there were tarps attached to several sections of the roof. Behind the house she saw several other dwellings, including one that had a perfectly beautiful cottage garden. She looked around and noticed several round yards, cattle pens, stalls with turnout areas, a huge barn and three tall windmills.

She sighed, finding it odd that for the first time, she wasn't thinking about how easily or quickly she might be able to make a sale should the place ever go on the market. Instead, she thought about how lovely it would be to live somewhere so beautifully idyllic.

She parked the car in the driveway and got out, looking around, hoping to find some sign of Jake, hoping it wasn't too inconvenient or inappropriate that she'd stopped by. She quickly called him, but it went directly to voice mail and she left a brief response, asking him to call her back if he wasn't too busy. She could hear music coming from the barn, and when she didn't get a reply after a few minutes Val grabbed her coat, slipped it on and then walked in that direction.

She spotted a young man, about nineteen, swaggering out from the barn, a saddle perched on one hip. "Hi," she said and managed a tight smile. "I'm looking for Jake Brockton. Is he here?"

The young man gave her a quick once-over, rubbed his whiskerless chin and half shook his head. "He's out musterin' strays with a coupla the guys. He left me here to clean some of the gear."

"I tried to call him," Val said and motioned to the cell phone in her hand.

He grinned. "You ain't gonna get no good reception from where they're at, ma'am. Too much rock."

The way he called her *ma'am* made Val feel about sixty years old. But there was a genuine politeness about the young man that was impossible to disregard, and she quickly thanked him and headed back to her car. She decided to check out the house and walked up the path and started heading around the side.

"Can I help you?"

The sound of a cheerful voice quickly grabbed her

attention, and she spotted a middle-aged woman walking the path from around the rear of the house. She was a tall, thin, fair-haired woman who wore jeans, a thick sweater and a long multicolored vest. A friendly-looking small dog stood at her side, and the woman was smiling.

"Oh, hi," Val said and took a right turn toward the other woman. "Actually, I'm looking for Jake Brockton."

The woman regarded her curiously, looked her up and down, tilted her head to the side, and then responded. "You must be Valene."

Val stiffened. "Ah...yes."

"I'm Lynda... Jake's mom."

Val felt both relief and embarrassment. She certainly hadn't expected to come face-to-face with his mother. She moved forward and held out her hand. "It's lovely to meet you. I was passing by here and thought I'd stop to see Jake. I called his cell, but it went directly to voice mail."

The other woman nodded. "He's out mustering a few strays down past the creek. There's a lot of rock around that way and it makes for poor cell reception."

"I met one of the hands by the barn and he said the same thing."

Lynda grinned. "That'll be Ricky. He's been working here a few months. Jake should be back soon. Why don't you come up to the house and I'll make tea?"

Val resisted the urge to check her watch. She had a later appointment at the office but could certainly spend some time with his mother. She nodded and followed the woman up the path. The dog wound itself around Val's legs, and she petted the animal on the top of the head.

"Jake's spoiled baby," his mother said and grinned. "Sheba?"

The dog barked at the mention of her name, which made Val smile. When they reached the cottage behind the house, Val stopped in her tracks. The garden was like something out of a fairy tale, with a well and small pond, plus rows of colorful shrubs whose survival defied any logic since it was winter and chillier than usual.

"Everything okay?"

Val nodded. "This is such a beautiful garden."

"Thank you," Lynda said and headed up the cobbled pathway. "My little piece of heaven. An English cottage garden in the middle of Texas. My daughter thinks I'm crazy for putting so much effort into it, but it makes me happy."

"How do you get these flowers and shrubs to grow?"

"Love and kindness," Lynda replied. "Plants really aren't all that different from people. They thrive on both of those things."

Val smiled and decided she liked Jake's mother very much, particularly when she discovered that the inside of the house was as adorable as the outside. From the mahogany furniture to the soft pastel accessories, the place was like something she'd seen on one of those old BBC shows about living in the English countryside. Val was tempted to grab her camera from the car and take a few snapshots.

"Your home is lovely," she said and half twirled around. "Jake said you've lived here for a long time."

Lynda nodded and moved into the kitchen. "Twenty years. My husband got a job as ranch foreman, and this cottage was where we lived. When he died so unexpectedly, I thought we might have to leave. Cassidy was still a child, and I was working a few days a week at the local elementary school. But then Jake came home, and everything worked out. And Cassidy was so happy she got to stay on the ranch." As she spoke Lynda moved around the small kitchen, gathering cups and filling the teapot.

There was a large framed sketch on the wall, of a herd of mustangs galloping through a creek bed, and Val recognized the strokes immediately. "Jake did this?"

Lynda nodded. "When he was about sixteen. He's very talented. And you work for your family's business, right?"

"Yes," she replied. "We sell real estate."

Lynda nodded again. "It's lovely when family can work together. You know, my son likes you very much."

Val's insides leaped. "I like him very much."

Lynda smiled. "He's been through a lot. Don't break his heart, okay?"

She was obviously referring to his last relationship, and as warnings went, it was mild and said with the utmost warmth. Val didn't mind. "I won't, I promise," she said and walked toward the fireplace.

There were several photographs on the mantel and she lingered over one that was of three men, one younger, one older and another older still, arms linked companionably at the shoulders. They all shared the same sandy-blond hair and glittering blue eyes. Jake and his father and grandfather. The picture made Val experience several different emotions. There was love and affection in the photograph, but she also knew it represented loss, of both his dad and grandparent. And suddenly it made her miss Glammy more than she usually allowed herself to. She knew how much Schuyler grieved the loss of their beloved grandmother, and Val made a mental note to talk more about Glammy to her sister.

"Is this your daughter? She's very beautiful," Val

said, moving to the next photograph of a young woman standing beside a tall palomino horse.

Lynda nodded. "Yes, that's Cassidy. My late husband, Mike, and I weren't expecting we'd have any more children after Jake since I had complications after the birth. But then along came Cassidy, and she has truly blessed our lives. And she adores her big brother."

Who wouldn't adore Jake, Val thought as she perused the photographs and then spotted one of Lynda and Jake. He was dressed in a cap and gown. He was younger, maybe midtwenties.

She frowned and pointed to the picture. "Jake's graduation?"

Lynda nodded proudly. "That was when he got his MBA. He worked so hard and graduated with honors."

Val's insides were suddenly and unexpectedly hollow. Jake had told her he'd dropped out of college. "He said he'd left school when his father passed away."

"He did," Lynda replied, her gaze narrowing a little. "But he went back to school online a year or so later. He's not one to boast or talk about himself. He gets that from his dad. My husband was a very humble and yet strong man. And he was such a wonderful father. And Jake will be the same," Lynda added, a gleam in her eyes.

Val swallowed hard, irritated and a little hurt by the fact that Jake hadn't told her about graduating college, particularly after Maddie had grilled him about it. Suddenly everything about him began to make sense. He was smart and articulate. He knew some of the people at the charity benefit. The young man she'd talked to by the stables clearly regarded him as an authority figure. He wasn't an uneducated hick. He was obviously more than a simple ranch hand.

And he had some serious explaining to do!

Chapter Eight

Jake knew he was in hot water the moment he entered his mom's living room. He wasn't sure how much his mother had told Valene—not too much, he hoped, because there were things he needed to tell her himself. Plus, he'd made it clear to his mom that he hadn't mentioned his money or owning the ranch to the woman he was dating. And although Lynda had warned him about the perils of deception, Jake was determined to see how his relationship with Valene progressed before he told her everything about himself.

Valene was sitting on the sofa in the small living room, sipping tea, and shot him daggers when their gazes connected. Seeing her in her work garb, and her hair in a neat ponytail, he remembered she'd told him she was meeting up with a client who lived close by, which should have registered the possibility that she would drop in at the ranch. Jake knew Otis McAvoy very well, since the older man had been a good friend of his father's. He noticed that his mother looked delighted that she was getting the opportunity to hang out with the woman who had taken up so much of his time and attention.

Jake kissed her cheek, saw his mother's approval and then sat down.

"Sorry I missed your call, but the cell reception can be a little hit or miss at times."

"I was in the neighborhood," she said flatly. "So I thought I'd come and see you. Is that okay?"

"Of course."

They all chatted for a couple of minutes, about the weather and the cottage and Sheba, who had perched herself at his booted feet, and once Valene finished her tea, she thanked his mother and stood up.

"I have to go," she said and collected her bag. "But thank you, Lynda. It was lovely to meet you."

"Likewise. Please come and visit again."

Once they were outside, she didn't wait for him, but charged down the path and circumnavigated the ranch house. The contractors were done for the day, but when Jake reached her, one of the young ranch hands passed by and smiled at Jake.

"Afternoon, ma'am. Afternoon, boss."

Jake saw her back stiffen, and when she reached the front of the house she turned, hands on hips. Her brown eyes were dark and her expression clearly unhappy.

"Your father's boots?"

"What?"

"Exactly," she shot back. "You told me someone had to fill your father's boots. At the time I thought you meant because of your mom and your sister, but it was more than that. You meant his job. He was the ranch foreman. And now you are. You're in charge here, right?"

Jake wasn't sure how to answer. He was in charge, so technically her assumption was correct.

"Yes."

"And you have an MBA?"

He nodded. "That's correct."

"And you didn't say anything about it because you don't like talking about yourself?"

"Something like that," he replied, seeing the fire in her eyes and suddenly itching with the need to kiss her. She looked so beautiful and it had been days since they'd been so close.

"It's really annoying how you do that, you know," she said flatly.

"Do what?"

"Make everything seem so damned reasonable. Drives me crazy. I really want to be mad at you right now."

Jake laughed softly. "Does that mean we get to make up and make out afterward?"

She crossed her arms. "Only if you show me inside this house," she replied, nodding at the ranch house. "If that's allowed."

"Sure."

He held out his hand and she took it, and a bolt of electricity raced up his arm. He wondered if he'd ever get used to that, or if the scent of her perfume would always stay with him for days after he'd held her in his arms.

Jake walked up the steps, crossed the wide veranda and opened the front door. Most of the furniture was covered in protective sheets, and any decorative items were safely stored in boxes. He'd started the renovation over two years ago and put a halt on it during the divorce. Since then, his mind had gotten clearer, and now he wanted the place finished so he could move back in and start his life over.

With someone like Valene...

It occurred to him that he'd never fallen so hard and so quickly before, and the realization made warning bells peal in his head. With Patrice, he'd spent high school desiring her, and when she had made her move, he had been flattered and a little relieved, thinking his search to find someone to share his life with was over. Of course, then she'd busted his heart into a thousand pieces and made a mockery of everything he'd believed they had.

"Wow," Valene said as they entered the hallway, taking in the raked ceilings, polished floors and wood accents throughout the house. "This is incredible. Are you sure the owners won't mind me looking?"

"Positive."

"Are they here?"

"Not they. He," Jake corrected. "And yeah, he's around."

"Well, if he ever wants to put this place on the market, let me know," she said and grinned. "Not that I want to put you out of a job by selling the place. But it's such a lovely home," she said as she traced her fingertips along the edge of the walnut newel post at the bottom of the stairs. "How long before the renovations are finished?"

"Another month or so, I should think. Would you like to see the upstairs?"

She nodded. "Love to."

Jake grasped her hand and led her up the stairway and down the hall. There were three bedrooms, one of which was a master suite with its own bathroom and small living area, and there was another bathroom that serviced both the other bedrooms. There was a balcony off the main bedroom that offered a fabulous view of the rear of the ranch, including the creek and the undulating pasture. The furniture was covered in sheets, and she lingered for a moment at the foot of the large four-poster bed. Jake stared at the intricately carved piece Patrice had insisted he pay a fortune for. He'd never liked it, thinking it too old-fashioned and heavy for his taste. Jake intended to ditch the bed, particularly since he'd discovered his ex-wife between the sheets with another man.

"This room doesn't look like it's been used in a while," she said.

"It hasn't," he replied.

She glanced around the room. "I'm guessing there hasn't been a whole lot of happiness in this house."

"Not especially," he replied. "Ugly divorce."

"That's sad," she said and walked out onto the balcony. "You know, I can't tell how many of those ugly divorces I've used to my advantage in the last year or so...you know, to get a client motivated for a quick sale. Sometimes I feel like a used furniture salesman scouring the death notices in the newspaper. What an amazing view," Valene remarked as she wandered around the perimeter of the balcony. "Is that an orchard?" she asked, pointing to the left.

"Pecans," he replied. "And not exactly an orchard, but there's potential, I guess."

When the cows began to bellow, she smiled. "It's so peaceful here. I'm not sure I would ever sell this place if it was mine. You're lucky to have spent so many years in such a beautiful spot. It must have been a wonderful experience to be raised here."

"It was. That's why I—"

"It's why you quit school," she said and turned to face him. "So that your mom and Cassidy could stay here. You did the job your dad used to do, so they wouldn't have to leave."

He shrugged. "This is home."

She moved in front of him and settled her hands at his waist, linking her thumbs through the loops on his jeans. It was an incredibly intimate gesture and one that had the temperature of his blood skyrocketing. Jake kept his arms at his sides, even though all he wanted to do was haul her close and kiss her.

"And then you went back to college and your mom said you graduated with honors," she said and sighed. "Jake, I'm sorry if I ever inferred that you were—"

"An uneducated hick more interested in peanut shells and beer than anything else?" he said, cutting her off. "No," he assured her. "You haven't. But I appreciate your apology."

She pressed closer. "Sometimes I put my foot in my mouth and say inappropriate things."

Jake wound his arms around her. "But I'll bet you have pretty feet."

She chuckled. "Actually, I do have nice feet. I'll have to show you sometime."

"I'm looking forward to it."

He kissed her and felt the breath sucked from his lungs like a vacuum. The moment her tongue wound around his, Jake was lost. She was like tonic, like air and food and everything he needed for sustenance.

"Jake," she whispered against his mouth. "Would you like to make love to me?"

It was a sweet, tempting invitation. One he fully intended accepting. "Absolutely."

"When?"

"Soon," he promised. "But first, I need to tell you—"

His words were interrupted by the sound of a cell phone ringing. She sighed and stepped back, removing her hands from his belt before diving into her handbag for her phone. The call lasted less than a minute and then she slipped the cell back into her bag.

"I'm sorry," she said quickly. "I have to go."

"Everything okay?" he asked, seeing the furrow between her brows.

"A family thing," she explained. "That was Maddie. She wants me to come to the office right away. Trouble at work."

Jake nodded, understanding immediately. "If there's anything I can do, let me know."

"I will," she assured him.

"And I'll see you Saturday?"

"Yes," she replied and kissed him softly on the mouth. "Thanks for the tour. And the kiss."

"I'll call you tonight," he said once they were back at her car. "Take care."

Jake watched her drive off, his heart unusually heavy. He hated seeing her out of sorts, and the phone call had definitely not been a good one. He was just about to turn on his heels when his mother stepped up beside him.

"She's a nice girl."

"I know," he remarked.

"But you don't trust her?"

Guilt hit him between the shoulder blades. "I'm not sure what I feel."

"She's not Patrice," his mother reminded him. "And I don't think she's the mercenary type. She comes from a wealthy family, so I'm pretty sure she isn't after your money."

"It's not that, Mom."

"I know," his mother said. "But you need to tell her the truth, before someone else does."

The first thing that Valene noticed when she returned to the office was the fact that the secretary at reception looked frazzled and barely acknowledged her. Maddie's earlier phone call had been fraught with tension and urgency, demanding her presence. She headed straight for the conference room and was stunned to see Schuyler standing by the window.

And her parents!

They weren't due back for another week, and Val immediately wondered what had happened to make them abort their vacation so abruptly.

"Mom! Dad!" she exclaimed and rushed directly toward them, delighted to see them both.

They embraced her affectionately, and she was certain her father clung to her longer than usual. When she stepped back, she noticed that Maddie and Zach were also in the room, along with her brother-in-law Carlo and her brother Everett, who looked particularly grim.

"What's going on?" she demanded.

"Trouble," Maddie said and sighed. "We lost the Butterworth account."

Val knew what that meant. Fortunado had been selling Butterworth property for close to two decades. Laurence Butterworth had been a family friend for just as long. Butterworth Industries was responsible for most of the residential development on the outskirts of the city—affordable, middle-class real estate that turned over quickly and was highly profitable for both the developer and Fortunado—as well as the commercially zoned development in the heart of town, which included Fortunado's exclusive listing for most of the shopping malls.

It was a huge blow. Butterworth was Fortunado Real Estate's most important client.

And the loss was one they might not recover from.

Val winced when her father thumped his fist on the conference table. "I'll be damned if I'm going to let decades of work go down the drain overnight. Someone is responsible for this."

"But who?" It was Schuyler who voiced what they were all thinking.

"I don't know," Kenneth replied, red faced. "But I'm sure as hell going to find out."

"We've hired a private detective to do some digging," Zach said and dropped a stack of files on the table. "These are the clients we've lost in the last three months. These," he said, dropping another stack of files, "are all the clients we think might be at risk. And this," he said for dramatic effect as he held up a piece of paper, "is a list of anyone we think might be worth investigating. Feel free to add names to it. The more people we look at, the better chance we have of finding out who is responsible."

Val wasn't interested in any cloak-and-dagger subterfuge, but she did want to know who was trying to ruin the family business. She also wanted to remain positive. "We've signed on a few new clients in the past couple weeks, like the Messer Group account, so surely that will help with the loss of Butterworth."

"Of course," Zach said. "But I don't think we can ignore the fact that someone is deliberately doing damage to this company. Which is why everyone we know needs to be put under the microscope."

"Like who?" Val asked.

"Like your new boyfriend."

Maddie's voice was filled with suspicion, and Val saw that her father was frowning. "Jake has nothing to do with this. We were losing clients a long time before I even met Jake. He works on a ranch, for goodness' sake, and he's certainly no threat to Fortunado Real Estate."

"You can't know that, Val," Zach said gently. "We can't leave anything or anyone to chance."

"Maybe he sought you out because he wants to get close to the family," Everett suggested. "You know, to get information."

Val was shocked by the intimation. The very idea that her family believed Jake might be using her for information about her family *or* be responsible for any of the disasters that had landed in the company's lap lately made her seethe. They didn't know Jake and they had no right to make assumptions.

"Please don't do this," she implored and then looked at her father. "Daddy, I'm asking you to respect his privacy and believe me when I say there is no way he is involved in this."

"Sorry, Val, everyone is a suspect," her father said calmly. "With everything that has been happening with us and with the Fortunes, we need to investigate everyone. Particularly after the fire at the Robinson estate and the fact that Ben Robinson was nearly killed. This is serious…too serious to waste time worrying about what your new beau might think is his right to privacy. I'm not taking any chances when it comes to my family."

Val's heart sank. She knew her father was relentless when it came to family matters. And since the business was part of the family, it became very clear that he believed they were in the middle of a full-on attack. It was made worse by the fact that she was still reeling from what she'd learned about Jake that afternoon, and she certainly didn't want her family poking around in his business. Jake was a private man and would not appreciate being investigated. On the other hand, there was no way she could tell him what was happening without being disloyal to her family.

She was at an impasse.

Which was exactly what she told her brother Connor when she called him at his home in Denver later that evening.

Out of all her siblings, Connor was the one she always leaned on for advice. He was a straight-talking, no-nonsense kind of man, and one who could be trusted implicitly.

"I don't know what to tell you, kid. You know how complicated this family is now," Connor said and laughed a little. "With the Fortune connection, we're bound to be a target for some unscrupulous characters. And if you think this new guy of yours has nothing to hide, what are you worrying about?"

"Because it's invasive and completely unnecessary." She sighed heavily. "I wish you were here to help sort this mess out."

"I will be," he assured her. "I'll be back in Houston in a few weeks."

Val made an excited sound. "Wonderful. I miss you. Mom and Dad miss you. But what brought on this upcoming visit?"

"I just need to talk to everyone in person about something."

"What?" Val asked, instantly suspicious. "Is something wrong? Are you okay? Should I be worried?"

"No, yes and no," he replied, answering her three questions. "You see, that's why I don't tell you and Maddie and Schuyler anything. You all jump to conclusions. I'm perfectly fine."

"I thought you might be getting married or something," she teased.

"Not a chance," he flipped back. "You know I'm not the marrying kind."

"You might be," she ventured, "if you meet the right girl."

"You're the one all caught up in this romance thing," he shot back and laughed. "Not me. This cowboy of yours has got you all hot and bothered."

"You're making fun of me."

"A little. Good night, kid. See you soon."

She ended the call, took a shower, fed Bruce and then heated up soup for herself. She played with the dog for a while, thinking that she had been ignoring him too much lately and hadn't been as strict about his walking and grooming. The truth was, she was out all day, every day, and she knew he must be lonely. Maybe he needed a friend. She had the room, and the yard was certainly large enough for another pet. She hopped onto her laptop and sent an inquiry email to the breeder she'd purchased Bruce from, and by eight o'clock, Jake called. They talked for about twenty minutes, about everything and anything and nothing in particular, and Val avoided saying anything about Fortunado Real Estate. He seemed unusually distant, and she wondered if he was annoyed that she'd dropped in unexpectedly at the ranch but was too polite to say anything. But when she asked him, he quickly brushed off her concerns. And when she reminded him that he'd said he wanted to tell her something before they were interrupted by Maddie's phone call earlier that day, he said they'd talk on the weekend.

As she drifted off to sleep later that night, Val tried not to make a big deal out of his evasiveness, or the guilt pressing down between her shoulders because she knew her father and Zach were about to start snooping into his life.

On Friday morning, the day before Valentine's Day, she received a box of heart-shaped cookies from the local bakery and knew immediately they were from Jake even though there was no note attached. An hour later, a bouquet of flowers arrived for her via a delivery service. They were cottage-garden flowers, the kind you would find in an English garden and not the kind ordered from a florist. The fact that he'd picked them himself and arranged for a courier to drop them off filled her heart with happiness. Again, there was no note or card, but she knew they were from Jake and she couldn't have imagined a more romantic gesture even if she'd tried. Realizing he knew she would prefer the wildflowers to something flashy and store bought, like roses or oriental lilies, amplified every feeling she had for him. It was turning out to be the perfect Valentine's Day weekend.

She stepped out of the office at midday, at Schuyler's insistence. After her sister had snooped around and noticed the flowers and cookies, she insisted Valene reciprocate and get Jake the perfect Valentine's Day gift. She loved spending time with her sister and was touched to know Schuyler always made time for her when she was in town.

"It's cute that he's sending you gifts today," her sister said. "I'll have to get Carlo to up his game. So, what do you think of this?" Schuyler queried, holding up a dark Aran sweater. "For my handsome husband? Or your hot cowboy?"

"Nice," Val said as she wandered around the small and exclusive men's boutique. "But it doesn't help me. I can't buy Jake a sweater. It's too soon for that. Besides, I don't know his size."

Schuyler raised her brows provocatively. "You will once you get his clothes off."

Val waved a hand, walked around the leather goods cabinet and spotted a tray of tie pins and slides. One of the slides caught her attention, and she asked the sales clerk if she could take a closer look. It was perfect, fine platinum edged in gold and engraved with a horse standing on its hind legs. She purchased the item immediately and had it gift wrapped while Schuyler went on behind her about how boring she was.

"So, where is soon-to-be lover boy taking you tomorrow?" Schuyler asked once she'd paid for the sweater.

"I have no idea," Val replied as they left the store. "He just said we'd be spending the day together."

"He certainly is romantic."

Val's skin warmed. "I know."

"Have you told him about the private investigator?"

She shook her head. "No."

"Divided loyalties, huh?"

She sighed. "It's difficult."

Schuyler nodded. "I imagine it would be. I remember when I was falling for Carlo, I was so wrapped up in him, so completely in lust, I don't think I would have been able to keep that kind of secret. But then, you've always been better at keeping your feelings under wraps than I have."

"You mean I don't wear my heart on my sleeve. I know, I'm uptight like Maddie."

Schuyler sighed. "No one is as uptight as Maddie, although she has mellowed some since marrying Zach. And you've always been the most considerate one out of all of us. You've never liked hurting people. Or keeping secrets. It's why we all love you so much."

Val's eyes burned. "I don't know what to do."

"What does your heart tell you?"

"That Jake is exactly what I've been looking for."

"Even though he doesn't tick all those boxes you were so hung up about a few weeks ago?" her sister asked as they walked through the door of the Fortunado building.

Valene shrugged. "You mean the money and the sophistication? I think those qualities are overrated. And actually, he's highly intelligent and articulate and—"

"I get the picture," Schuyler said, waving a hand. "But you must know that regardless of all the drama that's happening in the business right now, Dad would always want to check out anyone you started dating that he hasn't handpicked. When he called two days ago and said he and Mom were coming home early from their vacation and that he wanted me here, he also asked me if I'd met your new boyfriend."

"Jake's not my boyfriend," she corrected. "We hardly know one another."

"I think I knew Carlo about three days when I realized how much I liked him. It doesn't matter how long you've known him. Look at Maddie and Zach. It took them five years to admit how they felt about one another. But you and I aren't as cautious as that, Val. We're a little more free-spirited and less afraid than Maddie. Go with that. If you like him, then like him. You don't need anyone's permission other than your own."

Val was still thinking about her sister's words when

she left the building for the afternoon. Jake called at eight and they made arrangements for him to pick her up at nine the following morning. He instructed her to wear jeans and boots and, as expected, announced they were going horseback riding the next day.

"You know I can't ride a horse," she warned him as they headed to the ranch on Valentine's Day.

"I know, but you'll be perfectly safe," he said and grinned, looking gorgeous in worn jeans and a blue chambray shirt—the same shirt he'd worn on their first date at the coffeehouse.

"I like that shirt on you," she remarked and reached across to touch the soft fabric for a moment.

"This old thing." He smiled. "It's my lucky shirt."

"So, you're planning on getting lucky?"

He laughed. "I meant it brings me luck."

Val smiled. "Does it?"

"Well, I'm here with you, so I'd say it's working just fine."

Her heart rolled over. "You're very sweet."

"Sweet?" he echoed. "I'm not sure I've been called that before."

She laughed and then sighed. "It's so nice to relax and not think about work or anything else."

"Like what?"

"Fortunes or Robinsons," she replied and then gave a brittle laugh. "I don't want to bore you with the details."

"Nothing about you bores me, Valene."

Her heart rolled over, but she still didn't feel right about saying too much about what was going on with her family.

She shrugged lightly. "We've lost a few more clients, and it's at critical mass. My folks came home early from their vacation to try to sort things out."

He glanced sideways and she saw the concern in his expression. And something else. Wariness. "Is there anything I can do to help you?"

"Besides exactly what we're doing now?" She shook her head. "Not a thing. I'd just like to forget everything today."

"I'll see what I can do," he said quietly. "And I'll cook you breakfast in the morning."

Val was about to respond when she got the real meaning behind his words. "Oh…okay. My place or yours?"

"Yours," he replied. "Unless you want to spend the night in the bunkhouse. It can get a little crowded."

She chuckled. "My place it is, then. Besides, I'm sure Bruce is keen to see you again. I've been thinking of getting him a companion."

"Good idea. Puppy or rescue dog?"

"Puppy," she replied and then saw his brows shoot up. "Okay…rescue dog. See what a good influence you are?"

"I'm not sure you'd agree if you knew what I was thinking right now."

Val's skin warmed. "Then tell me."

"I want to turn this truck around, take you home and make love to you all day long."

She turned in her seat, noticing that his hands were tightly gripping the steering wheel. "Then turn the truck around, take me home and make love to me all day long."

"Don't tempt me," he said and cast her a long and sexy look.

Val laughed freely, feeling so completely at ease, so completely *in like* with him that she could barely contain her happiness. "I'm glad you wore that shirt today."

His brows rose. "Why?"

"Because it means we're both going to get lucky."

Chapter Nine

Jake tried very hard to concentrate on what he was doing for the following few hours, but it was damned difficult when everything that came out of Valene's mouth was flirtation and pure seduction. She had him at her mercy and he was pretty sure she knew it.

And he didn't mind one iota.

The air between them sizzled, fired up by the knowledge of how the day would end.

Once they were at the ranch, he took Valene straight to the stables and introduced her to her ride, an old chestnut mare called Agnes whom he trusted implicitly. Then he spent an agonizing twenty minutes standing behind her, explaining how to hold the reins, mount and keep her seat in the saddle. She was an excellent student, asking questions, not assuming she knew anything, and was clearly eager to get it right. But she was so close that every time she moved her hip would collide with his, which sent his libido skyrocketing like the space shuttle.

He'd given most of the ranch hands the day off and was pleased that they were making themselves scarce, except for Ricky, who made it his business to properly introduce himself to Valene and looked a little smitten. Not that Jake blamed the young man, since Valene was incredibly beautiful.

He led her into the small corral by the stables and got her to mount the horse, tucked her feet into the stirrups and, once she was holding the reins correctly, led her around the yard for a while until he believed she was confident enough to handle the mare out in the open. He quickly tacked up his gelding, attached a couple of saddlebags and checked over Valene one more time, which included making sure she wore a safety helmet. He clipped a long rein from her horse to his, then they headed off down toward the creek.

It was a picture-perfect day, cool, but the sun shone brightly and the sky was a vivid blue. She looked good in the saddle, too, he noticed, like she was born to ride. Her hips moved to the rhythm of Agnes's amble and she held the reins softly. She had a strong and well-balanced seat, and like with everything she did, she had purpose in her actions.

"Is that tether necessary?" she asked and pointed to the long rein connecting the two horses.

"Yep," Jake said and tipped his Stetson a fraction. "I'll take it off next time."

"How much trouble could I possibly get into?"

"Enough," he replied and motioned to the rocks and trees surrounding them. "I trust Agnes completely, but horses sometimes spook and I don't want you falling off and hitting your head on anything."

"I've got a tough head," she said and laughed, tapping the helmet.

"I couldn't bear it if anything happened to you."

As he said the words, Jake experienced a sharp pain in the center of his chest. Since his marriage had ended, he hadn't allowed himself to feel much of anything—not joy or humor or passion. But around Valene, he experienced all those emotions. And a couple of weeks ago he wouldn't have imagined it was possible to fall so hard and so fast. But he had. He liked her with an intensity that seemed at odds with the measured, calm and ordered way he'd lived in the past. Even with Patrice, he'd known exactly what he was doing. Marriage had been simply another step in the right direction, one that would lead to happiness and children and a lifelong commitment. Looking back, as much as he'd wanted her in high school, he hadn't spared her much thought until she reentered his life several years later. Courting her, marrying her, had seemed the logical thing to do. But with Valene, his usual controlled resolve had disappeared. For starters, he'd never considered himself the romantic type…but he was compelled to woo her in whatever romantic and sappy fashion he could think of. Because it made him feel good, and that had been in short supply during the last couple of years. And Valene, as passionate and vibrant as she seemed, was also something of an old-fashioned girl from an overprotective family and was worthy of all his attention, and not just so he could get her into his bed.

"Besides, your father would be after me with a shotgun if I allowed you to get hurt," he said, trying to lighten the mood.

But at the mention of her father, she frowned. "Jake,

about my dad…he's a good man, you know. And he always acts with the best intentions."

"Of course. I guess at some point I should meet you parents?"

She nodded. "I'm sure my mom would like that."

"And your father?"

"He's a touch more protective. I'm sure you'll be the same when you have a daughter."

Jake's insides contracted. After what had transpired with Patrice, children had seemed way out of reach. But now, not so much. Of course, it was way too soon to start considering that kind of commitment with Valene. But he liked knowing that he had hope in his heart again, and not just regret and pain.

Jake led them down toward the creek, conscious of keeping Agnes on the track. When they reached a tree near the edge of the water, Jake came to a halt and dismounted and then moved around to help Valene. Once she was on the ground, Jake tethered the horses and then helped Valene take the helmet off.

"I guess I have hat hair now?' she asked and laughed, fluffing out the waves.

"You look as lovely as always."

She reached up and briefly touched his face. "Thank you. What a magical spot," she said, hands now on her hips as she surveyed the area. "It's so beautiful."

Jake watched her, enthralled by the passion in her voice as she kept talking, and by the way she noticed everything, from the wildflowers to the birds to the gentle ripple of the water over the colored stones in the creek bed. Several head of cattle were drinking on the other side of the creek, and she ventured across a few rocks, her booted heels clicking over the stones. She stood alone, one hand up to shield her eyes from the sun, the other at her side, and he experienced a consuming feeling of attraction and longing that almost knocked him off at the knees. But it wasn't simply her physical beauty that attracted him…it was her intense zest for life. She'd grown up wanting for nothing, with an adoring family, the best education money could buy, fancy cars and luxury most people never knew. And yet something as simple as the bellow of a cow, the call of a bird or the sound of water rushing over rocks captured her attention in a way that was mesmerizing to witness.

She turned and met his gaze, smiling warmly. "Thank you for bringing me here. I'm so glad you got the day off today. Your boss must be—"

"Valene," he said, cutting her off. "There's something I have to tell you."

"I know," she said and skipped back across the rocks. "You sent me the cookies and the flowers yesterday. And they were lovely. Although," she said a little more seriously, "you shouldn't have wasted your hard-earned money on a delivery service. I would have been just as delighted to get them in person today."

Jake's gut dropped. "Valene, about the money. You know I—"

"I don't care about money, Jake," she implored, moving closer and resting her hands on his chest. "I never have. I care about *you*. More than I imagined possible. Everything you are—honest and strong and caring— that's the important stuff. That's what I want."

Guilt hit him directly in the center of his chest. *Honest.* Right… He really had to come clean. "Valene… I'm not without flaws, you know."

"I don't believe you," she said and smiled. "And can we ditch this serious talk and simply enjoy the moment?"

Jake considered his options. And he decided now was not the time to come clean. "Sure. Go and take a seat over there," he said and pointed to a large log by the edge of the creek. "I'll be back in a minute."

She strolled off and Jake headed back to the horses. He took off the saddlebags and rejoined her by the water's edge.

"What's this?" she asked, spying the saddlebags.

Jake extracted a small plastic container and two sodas from the saddlebag. "My mom made brownies yesterday. I snatched a couple for you."

She grabbed the box and dug in, laughing delightfully. "My absolute favorite thing in the whole world."

"I know," he said and wiped a smear of chocolate off her lower lip. Then he kissed her, softly, slowly, not asking for too much, not taking anything she wasn't prepared to give him freely.

They stayed like that for a while, eating brownies, talking, kissing, staring out at the creek. It was a sweet and lovely way to spend an idle couple of hours. About noon they rode back to the stables and he left instructions for Ricky to unsaddle and strap down both horses. He waited for a moment while Valene petted and hugged Agnes and thanked her for being such a trustworthy mount. His mother had gone out to her quilting class for the afternoon, and he ushered Valene into the cottage and made lunch for them both. Nothing fancy, just ham and cheese sandwiches, but she seemed content to simply sit on the counter stool and watch him, chatting about the horses and the creek and asking questions about the beef industry.

"So, you sleep in the bunkhouse?" she asked, drinking the coffee he'd made.

"At the moment," he replied, thinking he had the perfect opportunity to explain that he was only there until the renovations on the ranch house were completed. "Sometimes I stay with Mom, unless Cassidy is home from school." Before he could say anything more, she spoke again.

"I guess you used to live with your ex?"

He nodded. "Yes, I did."

"Would you consider moving in with someone else?" she queried, shrugging. "I mean, down the road…you know…after a while."

Jake stopped what he was doing, holding his sandwich in midair. "Of course. But the thing is, I could never live in the city. My work is here."

She nodded and smiled. "Well, after spending some time here, I can see that the city is not all it's cracked up to be. And I kinda like the idea of cowboy boots at the end of my bed. Maybe I'll buy a place around here," she mused and smiled. "Land prices are good. Did I tell you that I already have someone interested in that listing I got not far from here? The owner is a bit of a cranky pants, but I think he'll come around."

"I'm sure he will succumb to your charms."

She laughed delightedly. "Getting new listings is all that's keeping me sane at work these days."

"I take it things haven't improved?"

"We lost our most important client," she said on a heavy sigh. "It will have a huge impact on the business and my dad is convinced we're being deliberately targeted."

"What do you think?"

She shrugged. "My dad has good instincts. So does Zach. All I can say is thank goodness I managed to get the exclusive contract with that property developer— you know, Karl Messer. At least that will alleviate some of the financial burden on the agency."

Her admission rattled him a little. "Are things that grim?"

"I'm not sure. But we can't keep hemorrhaging clients. I mean, imagine if someone rustled all the cattle off this ranch. Would the owner remain solvent?"

"I'm pretty sure he'd be okay," Jake replied casually. "He's invested wisely in other things."

"He's obviously a sensible businessman. So is my dad, but a real estate business relies on selling real estate. No clients equals no income. But please don't say anything about this to anyone," she said quietly.

Jake nodded assuredly. "You have my word."

"Anyway," she said on a long sigh, "let's not talk about it anymore." She dug into her jacket pocket and pulled out a small box. "Happy Valentine's Day, Jake."

He opened the box and examined the tie slide. "It's lovely, thank you."

"You can wear it to the next charity dinner I rope you into."

"That happens a lot?"

"Now that my mom's back in town, I'm sure there'll be plenty of charity functions to attend. Speaking of which, I promised Florrie I'd be at the fund-raiser for the shelter next weekend. And now," she said as she rose from the stool and cradled his face in her palms, "I'd like you to drive me home."

He saw the desire shining in her eyes. "Really?"

"Really," she echoed. "Because as much as I like you in that lucky shirt, all I want to do right now is get you out of it."

Val had never considered herself particularly seductive or flirtatious—but being around Jake gave her a kind of sexual confidence she hadn't known she possessed. They left about twenty minutes later, after Jake had grabbed an overnight bag with a few personal items and a change of clothes. It seemed oddly mechanical and yet infinitely sexy, and as she waited for him by his truck, Val experienced a heady kind of longing that made her knees weak and her blood simmer. He hadn't touched her or kissed her since their make-out session by the creek, but the heat and awareness between them clung to the air. There was no mistaking it, no denying the inevitability of what was going to happen between them.

They didn't talk much on the trip back to her condo, nor when she opened the security gate and walked up the path and then headed inside. Bruce came to greet them at racing pace, tail wagging and tongue lolling. Val discreetly locked him in the laundry with his bedding and favorite toys and returned to find Jake standing in the middle of the living room, his overnight bag at his feet, looking sexier than any man had the right to look.

She glanced down at her jeans and shirt. "I think I'll take a shower." She took a couple of steps and then turned. "Are you joining me?"

His eyes widened. "Is that an invitation?"

"Absolutely."

He picked up his bag and wordlessly followed her down the hall. Strangely, her bedroom seemed smaller with the both of them in it. She'd never had a man in this bed before, as she'd moved into the place the week after she ended things with Hugh. Since then she hadn't been intimate with anyone.

She stalled at the end of the bed. "I haven't done this for a while."

"Me either," he said and dropped the bag. "But I'm pretty sure we'll make out just fine."

Val smiled. As always, he had a way of putting her at ease. "Birth control?"

He withdrew a box of condoms from his bag and placed it on the bedside table. "Got it."

She ditched her jacket and draped it over the chair in the corner of the room and then quickly closed the shutters. She flicked on the bedside lamp, kicked off her boots, removed her socks and returned to the end of the bed.

Jake hadn't moved an inch. He stared at her, long and blistering, and the desire in his expression fueled her confidence. She reached for the buttons on her shirt, ignoring her trembling fingers as she slowly undid them. Then he finally moved, pulling his own shirt free of his jeans and dispensing with the buttons quickly. His chest was spectacular, his skin like satin stretched over pressed steel, with a sexy smattering of blond hair on his pecs. Val swallowed hard, stepping backward, dispensing with her shirt and jeans with record speed as she made her way to the bathroom. The large shower could easily accommodate two people, and once she was naked, she turned on the water and stepped inside, waiting as steam filled the space. He joined her moments later.

Never in her life had she seen a man with more masculine angles, more muscle, more sinew and strength. He was perfectly proportioned, generously so, and she swallowed hard as her gaze lowered and then moved back up to his handsome face.

He looked at her, her face, her shoulders, her breasts, her waist, her hips and legs, and with every second of their visual connection, Val was drawn further into his world. He didn't touch her, didn't speak, didn't move, didn't do anything other than offer complete and un-adulterated appraisal as the water sluiced over them, creating an erotic image that would remain with her forever.

"You're so very beautiful, Valene," he said finally.

She stepped forward, making contact, feeling his skin, so hot and wet and so utterly desirable she almost buckled at the knees. He must have sensed her reaction, because his arms came around her, settling on her hips, urging her closer. And then he kissed her, taking her mouth in a wild and erotic way that defied anything she'd experienced before. With the hot water beating down on them, with their skin slipping against each other, with his big hands splayed against her hips, Val lost all coherent thought. His tongue was in her mouth, his desire undeniable, his passion for her like a potent force, and she longed for it, craved it, needed it like she needed air in her lungs. She wrapped her arms around his waist and slid them upward, feeling his muscles clench firmer with every stroke of her hands. And she kissed him back, hotly and passionately. She gave up her lips and her tongue and reveled in the feelings he evoked throughout her entire body. As he kissed her, he touched her breasts, rousing the nipples to life, placing his mouth there and driving her wild. And he touched her intimately and so expertly she had to lean back against the cool tiles for support, craving the release he incited in her. His touch was addictive, his caress firm yet gentle, and she couldn't get enough of him.

"We have to get out of here," he muttered raggedly against her mouth.

Val managed to garner some strength in her legs and quickly turned off the water. She passed him a towel and grabbed one for herself and took a few moments to dry herself before she padded back into the bedroom, unbelievably unselfconscious. She'd never been so at ease with a lover, so in tune, so…free. She'd never wanted to make love with someone like she wanted to with Jake.

Once they were on the bed, he took her into his arms, holding her head steady, gazing into her upturned face. "Tell me what you're feeling," he whispered.

Val reached up and pulled his head toward hers. "Happy."

He kissed her again, smiling against her lips. And he touched her. He made her scorch, he made her writhe, he made her ache. He traced his tongue across her nipples over and over; he ran his fingers along every part of her, finding unbelievably erogenous places Val had never known she possessed. He caressed between her thighs skillfully, drawing her higher and higher toward release, kissing her in time with the rhythm his fingers created.

And when she could stand no more of the incredible erotic torture he was bestowing, he quickly grabbed a condom, sheathed himself and moved over her, holding her head gently between his hands, kissing her mouth in a deeply erotic way that made her instinctively lift her hips to meet him.

He entered her slowly, not breaking their visual contact, and in that moment, Val realized what she'd suspected for the past week and now couldn't deny. She was falling in love with Jake. And the passion she felt, the connection she experienced with him, was real. It was intense. It was everything she had dreamed of.

She kissed him, saying his name, gripping his hips in a message as old as time, and he moved inside her, his body a part of hers, her body a part of his. The rhythm he created was steady, not rushed, not hasty or self-serving. It didn't take long for her to succumb, and she flew higher than she ever had before, feeling the white-hot rush of release sweep through her entire body as wave after wave of pleasure coursed through her. And then she felt him shudder and she held on, experiencing both power and acquiescence in the moment he found that same release.

He rolled over, his breathing hard, his broad chest rising up and down as he dragged air into his lungs. "Be back in a second," he said and swung his legs off the bed and then headed for the bathroom.

By the time he returned, Val had moved the coverlet down and ditched some of the pillows. He slid back into bed and pushed away the sheet she was suddenly desperate to have covering her nakedness.

"Oh, no," he said and kissed her soundly. "We're past the self-conscious stage, sweetheart."

"Easy for you to say," she breathed and traced her fingers through the slight smatter of hair on his chest. "You're perfect in every way. And I'm not."

He eased her onto her side and ran a hand along her hip. "You look pretty perfect from here."

"That's just your post-sex vision," she said and pouted a little. "In a couple of hours, you'll see things differently."

"In a couple of hours," he said as he rubbed his thumb gently over one budded nipple, "I intend to make love to you again."

Val moaned. "I've never had anyone make me feel like this before."

"Ditto."

It wasn't a declaration of love. It wasn't even close. But it was…something.

"I need to send a great big thank-you to the dating

app people," she said on a dreamy sigh. "You know, it's a Robinson Tech app."

"I know," he replied and kissed her, lingering a little. "I signed on, remember?"

She chuckled. "That's right, your sister's suggestion. I think I like your sister."

"Well, I'm sure she'll like you, too. Now," he said as he rolled her over until she was lying on top of him, "how about we stop talking about anyone else who's not in this room. And you can tell me exactly what you would like me to do, Ms. Fortunado, to make you happy."

Val's entire body thrummed. "This," she said, feeling his arousal, "makes me happy."

They made love again, taking time to stroke and touch and get to know each other, and Val knew she had never been as intimate or as close to another human being in her entire life. When he was inside her again, she was on top of him, feeling so sexy and powerful, so in tune with her entire body, she could barely get enough breath into her lungs. Jake gripped her hips, guiding her in a way that gifted them both the most mind-blowing pleasure and cemented in her mind and heart what she had suspected. She *wasn't* falling in love with Jake. She *was* in love with him.

Completely and irrevocably.

Afterward they slept for a while, and then Val slipped out of bed to make coffee. It was after six o'clock and they'd been in bed for several hours. She was behind the counter, wearing his lucky shirt, when he appeared in the doorway, in nothing but his jeans with the snap undone. Her libido did a crazy leap.

"Hey," she said and smiled. "Hungry? I have the

makings of a somewhat great pasta dish in my refrigerator."

He smiled. "Or we could order takeout from Toscano's."

Val glanced at the clock on the wall. "At this hour, and on Valentine's Day? I don't like our chances."

"Serge owes me a favor. You know, you look very sexy in my shirt."

She touched the fabric with idle fingers. "It's soft."

"Are you okay?"

"I'm fine. You?"

"Never better."

That was how she felt, too. As though she had finally found exactly where she wanted to be. And with whom. Well, not exactly where, because she knew that city living wasn't appealing to Jake. But Val wondered if there was a middle road for them.

He nodded. "I have something for you."

Her gaze roved up and down him possessively and then she grinned. "Something else?"

He laughed and then disappeared back into the bedroom for a moment. By the time he returned, Val had the dinner ingredients laid out on the countertop. He carried a small, flat parcel wrapped in bright pink tissue paper. There was a card attached, and she read that first. The sentiment inside was romantic and exactly what she would expect from a man like Jake. Val sat on a counter stool and opened the gift, sighing when she saw what he'd given her. A picture of herself and Bruce, sketched in intricate detail and beautifully showcased in a silver frame. She looked at the likeness, saw something in the expression he'd drawn, how he'd made her look good, and she glanced at him.

"Is this how you really see me? No little bump in my nose, no pointy chin, no flaws?"

"Exactly."

"Thank you," she said on a sigh. "I love it."

Jake moved forward and stood between her legs, settling his hand lightly on her shoulders. "What to get the girl who has everything," he said and rested his chin on the top of her head.

Valene inhaled the musky and intoxicating scent of him. "I don't have everything."

He reached down and grasped her chin, tilting her head backward. "No?"

She met his gaze. "Well, actually, at the moment, it feels like I do."

And as he kissed her, as their mouths met and he pulled her close, Val knew she had everything she'd ever wanted. His friendship. His body. His trust.

And, if she was lucky, his heart.

Chapter Ten

On Monday, life returned to normal. Sort of. Val was still in a kind of dreamy, post-Valentine's weekend of sensual bliss, recalling every romantic and passionate moment they had spent together, when Maddie popped her head around the doorway to her office at eleven o'clock.

"How was your weekend?" her sister asked.

Val looked up, smiled and felt heat scorch her cheeks. "Perfect."

"Really?" Her sister looked skeptical.

"I'm not going to pretend I don't care simply because I haven't known him very long."

"It's only been a few weeks," ever-practical Maddie reminded her.

"Some of us don't need five years to figure out who we want to be with," Val said pointedly. "Although we are all glad that you and Zach came to your senses and realized you were meant to be together."

Maddie's steep brows rose significantly. "Oh, I see... you're in love with Jake now?"

She didn't bother denying it. "Yes."

"And is he in love with you?" Maddie asked and stepped into her office.

Val shrugged. "I don't know. It's not like we've said the words or anything. But I feel... I feel very strongly about Jake."

Her sister's expression softened. "I hope he's everything you believe he is."

"He's more," Val assured her sister. "He's got integrity and strength, and he's so incredibly nice. As it turns out, I don't care about wealth or power or career. I care that he makes me laugh, that I feel like I'm my genuine self when we're together. That he's not judging me, not resenting me, not trying to get something from me, and not with me because we're from the same kind of family."

"Are you sure?" Maddie asked quietly.

"Positive. He's not after our money or our name. If you could see the way the people around him look up to him," she said and sighed, "you'd realize that Jake is very much his own man."

"You slept with him?"

She nodded. "And it was incredible. I've never experienced real passion, or desire, or real chemistry before. I mean, I've imagined feeling like this, but I never quite believed I'd find it. But with Jake I feel all of those things. Don't ask me to play the caution card, Maddie. It's not in my nature, and I like feeling this way."

When her sister left shortly afterward, Val got back to work, but her mind wasn't completely focused on the task. She took a call from Karl Messer and another from a potential new client in Austin she was seeing the following week. Despite losing the Butterworth account, Valene had never been busier. It was her time to shine, she thought. Her time to prove to her family that she could have a serious career and not simply playact. She knew that's what they thought. Oh, they loved and supported her too much to say so, but in her heart she knew none of her family truly believed she was cut out for business. She knew they figured she'd grow tired of the work soon enough and then get married and have a family. And maybe she would. Because the more she considered the idea of getting married and having babies, the more the notion appealed to her.

Beautiful little blond babies with glittering blue eyes. *Jake's babies.*

She sent him a playful text at lunchtime.

You're distracting me. V.

A few minutes later, her cell pinged in response.

I don't see how. I'm in the corral branding calves. J.

Val swooned over the heart emoji he added to the end of the message.

Call me tonight. V.

He did call, and they talked for half an hour, about random and mundane things. And she loved how they could talk about the simple stuff—even the weather— and it was still fresh and exciting.

She drove to Austin Tuesday morning for a meeting

and stayed the night, returning Wednesday. In the evening Jake came to her place and Val had every intention of making dinner. Until he kissed her and then she was lost. They made love quickly and passionately and she was stripped of every thread of self-control as she came apart in his arms. Afterward, they took a shower together and he helped her prepare dinner and she accepted that he was a much better cook than she was. Later, once the food was eaten and the dishes cleared, he suggested they watch a movie.

He even supplied the DVD. A zombie flick, one she hadn't seen.

"How did you know which one to get?" she asked as they snuggled on the couch, with Bruce doing his best to get into a comfy spot between them. In the end, the dog made do with his basket at the foot of the sofa. "This kind of movie isn't your thing."

He laughed. "My sister made a few suggestions. It's something you two have in common."

"What's that?" she teased. "That we're both crazy about you? Me especially."

He kissed her mouth. "You know, if there are any clowns in this flick, we're sleeping with the light on tonight."

"Oh, you think you're going to be sleeping," she said and turned, straddling him and moving her hips in a way that was deliberately provocative. "Not a chance."

As it turned out, there weren't any clowns in the movie, but Val quickly lost interest in watching once Jake began kissing her neck. They went to bed around ten, leaving the light on because he insisted on seeing her, and she experienced such acute and mind-blowing pleasure in his arms, Val thought she might pass out. There was something impossibly erotic about watching him reach the peak of pleasure, knowing she was giving him every part of herself, knowing every touch, every kiss, every slide of her hand and mouth were just for him. Just as his touch was for her alone. The night became a voyage of sensual discovery, of pleasure and release, and there were quiet moments of gentle vulnerability that filled her heart with so much love, she wasn't sure where he ended and she began. His every touch was like worship against her skin, every kiss was like a brand, every sigh a memento she would treasure forever.

In the morning they woke early and took the dog for a walk and then returned to eat breakfast together. He was ready to leave at eight, and she kissed him goodbye with the promise of seeing him Saturday morning at the shelter.

But he lingered in the doorway, looking down into her upturned face, his expression suddenly serious. "How about you come and stay at the ranch on Saturday night?"

She raised a brow. "Is that allowed?"

His blue eyes glittered brilliantly. "We need to talk, Valene, and I'd like to show you the ranch. I mean, really show you."

She pressed against him. "Like the hayloft in the barn?"

"Everything," he said and sighed heavily. "And what it means to me."

He sounded somber, not like his usual self, and she was immediately concerned. "Um…okay. Of course I'll stay. I'll take Bruce over to my parents for the evening."

They said goodbye, and she was already missing him by the time she returned inside and collected her bag and laptop. She wanted to tell him she loved him. Of course it was too soon. But the words burned on the end of her tongue. The condo seemed so much fuller with him in it, and standing alone in the living room now, Val realized how incredibly lonely she had been before Jake had entered her life.

He'd said they needed to talk and she was filled with anticipation and some fear. Talking sounded serious. Perhaps he was ready to admit that their relationship was headed to the next level—like real commitment. Or maybe he thought they were moving too fast? The notion that he might want to slow things down hurt more than bore thinking about. She didn't want to go slow—she wanted to jump headfirst into a serious relationship with him.

She'd been at work for less than half an hour when her father called her into his office. Even though her dad was retired, and Maddie and Zach were in charge, he still kept his office and used it on the odd occasion he was in the building. Val tapped on the door and entered the room, spotting her father immediately by the window, arms crossed, looking grimmer than she'd seen for a long time.

"Come in, Valene," he said and moved across the room to close the door.

"Is everything okay, Dad?"

He met her gaze, his brown eyes appearing tired. "Not exactly. I've discovered something that I would like to discuss with you."

"Something?" She frowned. "Do you mean you know who's responsible for us losing so many—"

"Sit down, Valene," he instructed.

Val stilled immediately and then took a seat. "Dad, what's going on?"

He took a breath and grabbed a thin folder from his desk. "You know your mom and I love you."

She nodded. "I know. I love you both, too."

"And you know I only want to see you happy?"

"Yes, of course."

He sighed heavily. "I want you to tell me everything you know about Jake Brockton."

Val rolled her eyes. "Not this again. I told you that Jake has nothing to do with what's been happening with the company and—"

"I know that," her father said quietly, cutting her off. "But please, answer the question."

She took a heavy breath. Okay, this was about her father being her *dad*. "You don't have to worry about me. I'm fine. In fact, I've never been better or happier."

"You seem happy," he said. "Answer the question, Valene."

She frowned. "Look, I know you have reservations, but I'll introduce you and Mom to Jake and you'll see that he is—"

"Answer the question," her father said again, firmer and more impatiently.

Val sat back in the chair. "He's very nice. We've been dating a few weeks. He works on a ranch near Fulshear. He's got a mother and a younger sister. He's kind and considerate and handsome and I like him very much. In fact, I more than—"

"Works on a ranch, you say?" her father queried, dropping the file in front of her. "Valene." He said her name with deliberate emphasis. "Your new beau, Jake Brockton, *owns* the Double Rock Ranch."

Val heard white noise so loud it screeched through her ears, then she thought about the absurdity of her father's words and laughed humorlessly. "That's ridiculous, Dad. Jake *works* on the ranch. He quit college when his father died and took over the job as foreman and studied for his degree online a few years later to get his MBA."

"That much is true," he father said and pointed to the file. "It's all in there. It also documents how he purchased the Double Rock Ranch eight years ago and has turned it into a very successful and highly lucrative business."

The white noise returned. "That doesn't make sense. What are you saying, Dad? That Jake is—"

"Wealthy," he supplied. "Very wealthy. In fact, he's so wealthy that at the moment he could probably buy us out ten times over."

It made no sense. Val kept shaking her head, refuting her father's claims. "I don't believe this."

"Believe it," he assured her. "I have no reason to lie to you about this, Valene. However, your boyfriend is another story."

Val's insides ached. "It can't be true. Jake wouldn't deliberately deceive me. Why would he pretend to be a penniless ranch hand?"

"It might have something to do with the fact that his ex-wife took him to the cleaner's in the divorce."

Ex-wife?

Val wanted to throw up. Jake had been married? He was wealthy? He had lied to her over and over? It couldn't be true!

The look on her face must have given her away, because her father quickly responded.

"You weren't aware he'd been married?"

She shook her head. "I thought he had an ex-girlfriend."

"An ex-wife," her father amended. "A pregnant ex-wife, in fact. Take a look, it's all in the investigator's report."

A pregnant ex-wife?

Could he have stooped any lower?

The sickness in her belly reached her heart and she stared at the damning file, refusing to open it up and look. She didn't want to hear any more, because none of it made any sense. Why would Jake lie to her? Why would he pretend to be someone he wasn't?

"I'm sorry, kiddo," her father said quietly. "This wasn't what we were looking for when we started this investigation. It's just a little collateral damage, I'm afraid."

Had he really just equated her relationship with Jake to collateral damage?

Val grabbed the file and left the room without saying another word to her father. What could she possible say to assuage the humiliation and embarrassment coursing through her veins? There was no logical reason, no explanation Jake could offer that would undo the betrayal she felt. While she had been going on about gold diggers and money not being important to her, what a great laugh he must have been having at her expense.

When she returned to her office, she slammed the door and dropped into her chair. She noticed two unread text messages on her cell phone from Jake.

Lying, deceitful rat!

She ignored the messages and looked through the file, flicking through the pages with furious fingers.

Multimillionaire, divorced, baby with his ex-wife.

The list of his sins kept getting longer and longer.

She remembered the conversation they'd had in the upstairs bedroom at the ranch. The owner had gotten the place in an ugly divorce, he'd said. While that might have been true, he'd neglected to tell her *he* was the owner! He must have been laughing his ass off behind her back the whole time he was trying to get her into bed. Because that's clearly all they were about—the wildflowers, her favorite bagel, the sketches of her beloved dog, the trip to the animal shelter, the horse-back riding, the agonizing wait for his first kiss...the man certainly had the seduction thing down to a fine art. What was worse, he knew how important honesty was to her. She'd told him, when they were wrapped in each other's arms, how difficult it had been to learn to trust again after Diego's blatant disregard for her feelings once she'd discovered he was only interested in the Fortunado name and money. What a gullible and utter fool he must think her to be.

Jerk! Jerk! Jerk!

She hated him.

"Hey, sis?"

She looked up, not realizing she was holding her head in her hands. And also not realizing she had tears on her cheeks. Maddie stood in the half-open doorway, her expression filled with compassion and worse, pity.

"I know, you told me so, right?" she said and shrugged. "You said not to trust him, and I didn't listen and now—"

"Don't blame yourself," Maddie said gently and closed the door. "You didn't know he was pretending to be someone he wasn't."

Val scowled. "Why would he do it? Why act like a poor man when..." Her words trailed off and she gave a brittle laugh. "He took me to Toscano's for our first real date. I asked him how he managed to get a reservation on such short notice, and he said he knew the owner through the beef business. *His* beef business. He picked me up in a brand-new truck the night of the charity benefit, and when I asked him who owned it, he said it belonged to the ranch. *His* ranch. He gave me a tour of the ranch house that's being renovated and said the owner had been through an ugly divorce. *His* ugly divorce. And there's a child," she added, her rage gaining momentum. "He has a *child* and he didn't tell me. And I...I fell for it... I fell for his sexy, workingman charm, and within a couple of dates I was putty in his hands. I fell in love with a man I know *nothing* about, Maddie. Everything he said to me was twisted around and manipulated and said for a purpose—because he wanted to deceive me into thinking he was someone else—someone with values and integrity and honor. I feel like such a complete fool. And a condescending one, at that, because I know there were times over the past few weeks when I said things that made me sound like a spoiled snob. And all this time he was probably laughing at me."

"Perhaps there's an explanation," Maddie said, clearly trying to be a voice of reason.

Val shook her head. "There's nothing he can say to me that will erase the lies."

Maddie sighed. "What are you going to do, Val?"

She took a breath and squared her shoulders. "I'm going to do what I should have done the first time we met. I'm going to tell him to go straight to hell!"

Jake was standing in front of the house on Friday morning, listening to the drywall contractor complain about unreasonable time frames to get the place finished when he spotted Valene's car coming down the driveway.

He hadn't spoken to her the evening before. Instead she'd sent a text message pleading a headache and promising she would talk to him the following day. He certainly hadn't expected to see her. But he wasn't unhappy. All he needed to do was get the contractor to stop talking.

"Okay, okay," he said and held up his hand. "Another week, but that's it. I want it finished and your crew out of here by the end of the month."

He turned and walked down the path, greeting her as she pulled up and turned off the engine. She got out and as always, his heart skipped a beat. She looked tired, he thought, as though she hadn't slept, and he wondered if she was still struggling with a headache.

"Hey there, this is a nice surprise." He bent his head to kiss her and she twisted unexpectedly, so he only managed to feel her cheek beneath his mouth. "Everything okay?"

She looked up, her brown eyes darker than he'd ever seen them. "Perfect. Things have never seemed clearer."

He noticed she was wearing her work attire, as though she'd come directly from the office, and her hair was up in a tight ponytail. "Valene, I—"

"I was wondering if you could show me around some more," she said and took a few steps toward the house. "You know, give me the full tour experience. Take me into every room of the house, and every stall and stable. I mean, I know you'd planned on giving me the full tour tomorrow, but since I'm here," she said and held up her arms, "how about right now?"

The tone of her voice sent alarms bells ringing, and since the tension emanating from her was palpable, it took him about two seconds to figure out what was wrong.

She knows...

"Valene," he said quietly. "Let's go inside and—"

"Inside?" she said shrilly. "Inside where? The bunkhouse? Your mom's house? The ranch house? Oh, hang on," she said and pointed to the house. "I mean, *your* house."

The air sucked from his lungs. "I wanted to tell you."

"When?" she demanded. "On our first date? Our second date? The first time you kissed me? The first time you got me into bed?"

It was then that he realized they had an audience. His mother, for one, and several of the contractors who were trying to look uninterested from their spot on the scaffolding.

"Let me explain," he said quietly.

"Explain what?" she shot back. "That you're not a penniless ranch hand?"

"I never actually said I was. You just assumed I—"

"I made an assumption based on what you told me," she said angrily. "On what I believed was the truth. The fact that nothing you have said to me so far *is* the truth makes it very clear what you think of me and this thing between us."

Jake could see the hurt etched on every line on her face. "I know I deceived you, Valene, but it wasn't ever intentionally malicious. And I tried to tell you several times about the ranch, but it—"

"I must have missed that part," she said, cutting him off. "And the part about your ex-wife!"

"Okay," he said, exasperated. "I also should have told you about Patrice. But frankly, it didn't seem important."

She laughed. "Not important? What about the baby, Jake? I guess that isn't important, either?"

His gut clenched. "It's not what you think."

"I don't believe it matters what I think. If it did, you wouldn't have been lying your ass off to me for the past three weeks."

He understood her anger, but it still annoyed the hell out of him. She wasn't listening. She wasn't even *trying* to listen. "I planned on telling you tomorrow night."

"Too little, too late."

Irritation curled up his spine. "That's an immature response, Valene. Yes, okay, I'm wealthy. I bought this ranch eight years ago, and with a lot of hard work I've made a lot of money, some that I've invested, some I've given to charity. And yes, I was married and now I'm divorced. And yes, my ex-wife *was* pregnant when we separated. But none of that," he emphasized, "has anything to do with you and me."

She shook her head, clearly bemused. And furious.

"It has everything to do with you and me," she shot back. "I trusted you."

"I know. I'm sorry."

"That doesn't cut it. Because I believed you trusted me, too. But I can see that clearly it was a one-way street. You had your own agenda and I was too gullible and naive to see it for what it was. I have to hand it to you, Jake, you gave a damned fine performance of being a humble ranch hand—right up to the cowboy dancing and wildflowers."

"It wasn't a performance, Valene. It was real, all of it. And the money doesn't change who I am."

She didn't look convinced. "Well, it shouldn't…but I'll never know, will I? You duped me. You made me believe you were someone you're not, and at times you made me feel small-minded and spoiled and overindulged. I've admitted things to you about myself that I've never told anyone, and as I was driving over here to say goodbye to you, it occurred to me that you really didn't let me get to know much of you at all."

Jake's belly took a dive. What was she saying? "Goodbye?"

"Yes," she replied. "I don't want to see you again."

"You're not serious."

"I'm perfectly serious."

Jake ran a hand through his hair, ignoring the fact that his mother and the contractors were in earshot and could probably hear every word they were saying. "So, we had a fight. We'll get past it."

She shook her head. "I don't want to get past it, Jake. And I'm pleased that I found all this out now, before I got in too deep. Have a nice life."

She turned and opened the car door, flinging it wide for effect.

"Valene…sweetheart, would you please let me—"

"I told my sister I was going to tell you to go to hell," she said and started the ignition. "But I can't want that for you, because I care too much. Damn you, Jake," she said, her eyes glistening with tears. "Damn you for making me fall in love with you."

Then she slammed the door and drove off down the driveway. Through the gates.

And out of his life.

"You just going to stand there," his mother said from behind him, "or are you going after her?"

Jake thrust his hands into his jacket pockets. "You heard her. She said goodbye."

His mother came up beside him. "I heard a very unhappy girl say that she was in love with you."

His insides clenched. "If that was true, she wouldn't have left."

"She's hurting. People act irrationally when they are hurt."

"Valene's in love with the idea of being in love,"

he said, watching her car disappear into the distance, aching all over. "You don't fall for someone in three weeks."

"I did," his mother said. "I knew I loved your father the first time we met. It was a blind date."

"I know the story, Mom."

"And you know how it played out," she reminded him. "We were married seven weeks after we first met. We had two wonderful children and twenty amazing years together. And I still miss him every day of my life."

Jake's throat tightened. "I know you do."

"I don't regret one moment. Losing him was devastating, but I know I wouldn't feel this intense grief if I hadn't experienced such a great love."

Jake sighed heavily. "What's your point, Mom?"

"You've allowed what happened with Patrice to damage your heart, Jake. You've fallen for Valene and you are too afraid to admit it."

"I'm not afraid of anything," he said quietly. "I simply don't believe that falling in love happens overnight. It takes time and—"

"Who are you trying to convince?" his mother queried. "The rest of the world, or yourself?"

It was a question he couldn't answer. He only knew he hurt all over.

And had no idea what he was going to do about it.

Chapter Eleven

Val had no desire to see Jake on Saturday. But she'd promised Florrie she'd be at the shelter to help out with the fund-raiser, and she wouldn't go back on her word. She spotted his truck in the parking lot. His new truck. Not the old Ranger he'd driven almost every time she'd seen him. Seeing the cherry-red vehicle inflamed her already fuming temper.

And her broken heart.

She'd spoken to both Schuyler and Maddie at length the night before, Schuyler pointing out Jake's many good points, despite his obvious deception. Maddie wasn't quite so forgiving, but even she tried to be more neutral than usual, no doubt because she knew Val was hurting so much. But Val wasn't hearing any of it. He'd lied. End of story. Schuyler, as expected, was more flexible and suggested she talk to him. But Val wasn't going to be manipulated any longer. She'd made her decision.

They were over.

She grabbed the gift basket she'd put together as a raffle prize and headed toward the tent near the entrance. Florrie was there, handing out instructions to the volunteers. A couple of dozen temporary pens had been erected for the dogs going up for adoption, and several cat cages had been set up underneath one of the tents. There was a face painter, some rides for the little tots and several craft stalls.

"Good morning," Florrie greeted her with a wide grin. "I think we're in for a busy day. I'm going to set you up in this tent to collate the adoption applications as they come in. Let's keep our fingers crossed that Digby finds his own special family today."

Val's already vulnerable emotions were pushed to the edge. Poor unwanted Digby. She swallowed the lump in her throat, took a deep breath and plastered on a wide smile. "I'll keep my fingers crossed. So, show me what to do."

Ten minutes later Valene was set up under the tent and had another one of the volunteers, Cam, a young man in his midtwenties, for company.

People started arriving, milling around the pens and strolling past the stalls. She sold raffle tickets and gave out information leaflets, and it wasn't long before she processed her first application for a mixed-breed puppy. She was laughing with Cam when she spotted Jake striding down past the dog pens, with a couple of large bags of dog food piled on one shoulder. He dropped the food in the tent and came around the side of the table, where he squatted beside her.

"Good morning, Valene."

She glanced his way and shrugged. There was nothing good about being forced to spend time with him. "Hello."

"How are you?"

"Fine."

He moved closer. "Can we talk privately?"

She pushed back her shoulders. "I'd rather not."

Cam clearly sensed the tension between them, because he was on his feet in a microsecond and quickly excused himself, making himself useful at the dog pens by chatting with prospective adopters and leaving her alone with Jake.

"Valene, please look at me."

She took a breath and met his gaze. "What?"

"I wasn't expecting you to turn up today."

"I made a commitment to Florrie," she said stiffly. "And I like to think of myself as someone with honor."

It was a direct dig, and they both knew it.

Humiliation burned her skin. She'd told him she was in love with him. God, it was too embarrassing to bear thinking about.

"Would you let me explain?"

"No."

He made an exasperated sound. "You just plan on staying mad at me?"

"Yes."

She *was* being childish, but Val was too hurt to care. She wanted to cry and hate him for all eternity. She'd spent close to forty-eight hours thinking about his lies, his ex-wife, his child and every other truth he hadn't had the decency to come clean about.

He stayed where he was for a moment and then exhaled heavily before straightening and walking off, his shoulders tight, his hands clenched at his sides. Even when she hated him, Val was still achingly attracted to every wretched inch of the man. He looked so gorgeous in his jeans, shirt and sheepskin-lined jacket.

"Never let the sun go down on an argument."

Val turned her head and saw Florrie standing behind her, a curious expression on her face.

She shrugged. "It's complicated."

"Love usually is. But I've known Jake for a long time, and I don't think I've ever seen him as happy as he's been the last few weeks. By my reckoning," Florrie said and grinned, "that's all your doing."

It was a nice fairy tale. But the older woman didn't know the details, and Val wasn't about to admit to anything. She didn't have a chance to respond, because Florrie spoke again.

"He had a hard time with that wife of his. She was bad news. Especially what she put him through with the baby." The older woman sighed thoughtfully. "He really would have taken care of the child. But she knew what she was doing right from the beginning. Hateful woman. He was heartbroken for such a long time."

Val could barely get air into her lungs. She didn't want to hear about Jake's ex-wife or his child or how broken his heart was. She didn't want to *feel* anything. At least, she didn't want to feel anything other than anger and rage, because that's all that was keeping her from crying every single second of the day.

Thankfully, Cam returned with a family looking to adopt one of the older dogs. Not Digby, unfortunately, and after a couple of hours Val walked to his pen and spent some time with the dog. He was such a sweet-natured little thing and clearly adored company. She was closing the door to his pen when she heard Jake's voice.

"I see no one is interested in him."

She glanced sideways and wrapped her arms around herself. "No."

Jake reached into the pen and picked the dog up. "He'll find the right family one day."

The pooch licked Jake's face and he laughed, the sound sending goose bumps across Val's skin. "Not everyone gets their happily-ever-after."

"That's a grim view of things," he said and petted the dog's ears.

"I guess I'm in one of those moods."

"Can I call you later?"

Val's mouth flattened. "No."

His brows rose. "Can I text you?"

"No."

"Can I send a raven?" he suggested and smiled, using a line from *Game of Thrones*, one of her favorite television series.

Val planted her hands on her hips. "No calls, no texts, no ravens. I told you that we were over, Jake," she said and realized that just saying his name hurt.

"You said you were in love with me," he reminded her. "Did you mean it?"

"Of course not," she refuted, hating that he'd brought her admission into the conversation. "I was confused and angry and—"

"You can avoid me, Valene," he said, cutting her off, "if that's what you really want to do."

"That's exactly what I want."

"I don't believe you."

She glared at him. "I don't lie, Jake. That's your department."

Then she walked off.

"Mom said you screwed up big-time."

Jake glared at his sister. Cassidy had the bad habit of saying whatever was on her mind, whenever the mood took her. And all her attention had been focused on him for the last ten minutes. She'd arrived at the ranch half an hour before and met him at the top of the stairs in the main house.

"Just leave it alone, okay?"

She shrugged. "Have you tried talking to her?"

He'd tried. Several times. He'd sent flowers. He'd sent text messages. And nothing. It was as though she'd wiped him from her memory.

"I wish you and Mom would stop gossiping."

"Can't help it. But I can help you," Cassidy said and grinned. "Let's have a look at your profile on the dating app and—"

"Forget it," Jake said, holding up his hands. "No more dating apps, no more dates, no more interfering in my life, okay? Next time I want a date, I'll find one the old-fashioned way."

Cassidy made a face. "Jake, you're so old-school and out of touch. This is how people meet each other these days. We're all busy, we're all trying to juggle careers and school and home life and friends and family. Things like this app simply speed up the process, that's all. Stop being such a stick-in-the-mud about it. If we set your profile back up on Perfect Match, soon you'll have—"

"I don't want to date anyone else, okay?"

"Anyone else?" she queried. "You mean, anyone other than Valene?"

Busted. His sister was too smart for her own good. "I'm not ready."

Cassidy's expression softened. "You really like her?"

Jake nodded. "I do."

"Is she ever going to forgive you?"

He shrugged. "It doesn't seem likely."

"I'm sorry, Jake."

"Yeah, kid, me too."

* * *

It was almost a week later, on Friday afternoon, when Jake headed into Houston to meet with his accountant. He'd been planning for some time to expand the business into Austin, and after spending all week crunching numbers, he decided he could certainly afford to take the chance now. After a productive meeting, he drove directly to the Fortunado Real Estate building.

"Jake?"

Maddie Fortunado-McCarter greeted him in the reception area a few minutes after he'd asked to see either her or Zach McCarter.

"Hello, Maddie."

She looked as guarded as always. "Val's not here. She's doing an open house and then going home afterward."

"It's you I'm here to see," he said swiftly. "Business."

One brow rose, and he remembered how Valene did exactly the same thing. In Maddie's office, twenty minutes later—after a conversation with Maddie and her husband—Jake nodded in agreement.

"Okay, sounds good."

"Val isn't going to be happy about this," Maddie remarked and keyed a few more notes into the laptop on her desk. "She hates you at the moment. With good reason," she added.

Jake wasn't about to get into a conversation about his and Valene's relationship with any of her relatives—as least, not until he spoke to her first. "It's business."

"Are you sure?" Zach asked.

"Do you mean am I sure I would have walked through the door of this building and not one of your competitors' had I not known Valene?" He shrugged. "I think so. Your company has a good reputation. And if you can get me what I want, where I want, for the price I want, then we have a deal."

The other man nodded and shook his hand. "I'll get right on it."

When Jake left, he stopped by Toscano's and ordered some takeout and then drove to Valene's condo, hoping she was home. She was. But she clearly had no intention of letting him in. Or having dinner with him.

"I have a date tonight," she said through the speaker system at the gate. "Go away."

"Please, Valene, I'd like to talk to you. Just talk. And after that, if you want to end things, then I will respect your decision."

Silence stretched between them like brittle elastic. Then she spoke. "Just talk?"

"Yes," he said quickly. "And eat dinner. I picked up Toscano's and I thought – "

"You thought wrong," she said frostily. "Go away."

Jake took a long and steady breath. "Please, Valene?"

Her heard her sigh, feeling her unhappiness through to the marrow in his bones. Then she spoke. "Okay."

Minutes later he was standing on her doorstep.

He held out the food as he crossed the threshold and Bruce came racing down the hallway.

"Make it quick," she said, taking the bag and heading to the kitchen. She placed the food on the countertop and crossed her arms tightly. "Talk."

Jake managed a smile. "You don't want to eat?"

"I told you I had a date."

His gut clenched. "Seriously?"

She nodded. "I didn't realize I needed your permission."

"You don't," he replied and swallowed the ache constricting his throat. "I just thought…"

"What?" she shot back. "That I would sit around moping? Wishing things were different? Pining after you?"

"I've missed you this week," he admitted.

"You mean you missed your weekly sleepover?"

"This isn't about sex," he retorted. "I miss talking to you. I miss our friendship."

"Friends don't lie to each other," she said hotly. "Friends don't make each other feel like a fool."

"If I did that, it wasn't my intention."

She didn't look convinced. "I must have sounded like an entitled snob to you—asking you if you had a suit, making comments about your old truck, acting as though I had any kind of clue what it's like to live paycheck to paycheck. What a joke I must have been to you. I insulted you every time I opened my mouth and I didn't even know it. But you did. That's quite the power play, Jake. I bet you play a good game of poker."

Even angry with him, she looked so passionate, so beautiful. It was everything he liked about her. Everything he *loved* about her.

Because he *did* love her.

Maybe it was too soon. Maybe he was crazy for allowing himself to feel something so intense after such a short time. But he didn't care.

And she deserved his truth, even if she didn't want to hear it.

Jake walked into the living room and sat down, pressing his hands onto his knees. He waited for her, hoping she'd sit beside him, but she chose a seat across the room. Finally, he spoke.

"Nothing about our relationship is a joke to me, Valene."

"I don't know how to believe anything you say."

"You can," he assured her. "Because you *know* me."

She looked uncertain. "Do I?"

"All right, you want the truth, here it goes. I was married," he said heavily. "For a few years. Her name was Patrice. I knew her in high school, but back then she never looked in my direction. I was working class, blue collar, and her father was a lawyer and she was part of the it crowd. But I noticed her. I was young and she was beautiful…but sort of cold, like one of those mannequins in a department store. When school ended I went to college and put all thought of Patrice out of my mind. And then my dad died," he said and let out a long and painful breath, "and I had to go home. The people who owned the ranch would have made my mom and Cassidy leave."

He paused, sensing she wanted to say something.

"That seems harsh."

"Just the way things are." He shrugged. "I came home and started working as a ranch hand, and in a year or so I was made foreman. My dad had left an insurance policy, which my mom invested and I worked a second job packing shelves at a store not far from the ranch. I studied for my degree and waited for the opportunity I sensed was coming. It happened when the owners said they were selling. I knew my mom didn't want to leave, and Cassidy was still in school. So I got a mortgage and with Mom's help I bought a ranch at a ridiculously low price because it had pretty much been insolvent for the previous decade."

"That's quite a risk," she said quietly.

Jake shrugged. "I had to try. My family was at stake."

"And the business?"

"I got lucky. I made a few good decisions and found a place in the market for a high-end product. I invested well, and in a couple of years the ranch was financially viable."

It was a gross understatement. Jake had made his first million within two short years.

"And then?" she asked.

"Patrice came back into my life," he supplied. "Only now I was successful enough to get her attention. But the marriage was a disaster, and neither of us was ever happy. It turned out that her father had a gambling problem, and I bailed him out more than once. And Patrice had her own demons. She demanded we renovate the house, so I agreed. Frankly, at that point I was prepared to do whatever I could to help salvage our marriage. But nothing was ever good enough. She went through money like it was water."

"Is that why you divorced her?"

He sighed. "I divorced her because I found her in bed with one of the contractors I'd hired to renovate the house."

Valene gasped and placed her hand to her mouth for a moment. "How despicable."

The pain and memory from those days had lessened with time, but the muscles between Jake's shoulders still twitched. "Like I said, Patrice had her troubles."

Silence stretched between them, and Jake forced himself to remain on the couch. He wanted to touch her so badly, to hold her in his arms and feel the tonic of her touch through to his very soul.

"And your child?"

A sharper, more intense pain twisted in his chest. "Not mine."

"Then why did Florrie tell me you would have raised the baby?"

"Patrice told me she was pregnant after we separated," he explained. "I'm certain she hoped it would mean a reconciliation."

"But that's not what you wanted?"

"God, no," he replied. "I've never believed that monogamy is a big price to pay when you're in a committed relationship. So for me, it was a deal breaker. But I would have raised the child with her, even though we weren't together anymore. However, that's not what she wanted to hear. That's when she said the baby wasn't mine and that she'd only married me for my money. She said that it didn't matter how big my bank balance was, I would always be working class. And that I would never be good enough for her. That I would never be successful enough. Never rich enough. After that, what ensued was a very bitter and very ugly divorce that cost me a lot of money and my pride and eventually robbed me of my ability to trust anyone."

It was the first time he'd admitted it out loud. And the first time he'd told anyone other than his attorney how bitter and recriminatory things had become between himself and his ex-wife. But he wanted Valene to know what he was feeling. And why he'd kept the truth from her about the ranch and his considerable wealth.

Val stared at him, feeling the connection between them with a blistering intensity. Her head was jumbled with so many emotions—compassion and understanding and then rage and resentment toward the woman who had hurt him so badly.

But that still didn't absolve Jake of his decision to lie to her.

"And the child?" she asked.

"She lost the baby. The last I heard she was living in New Orleans."

"She broke your heart?"

He shrugged. "More like my spirit."

Val pressed her knees together. "Why are you telling me this now?"

"Because you wanted my story."

"I wanted your story weeks ago," she said and got to her feet. "Before the feelings started."

"I couldn't," he admitted. "I didn't know you well enough. I didn't know if I could trust you."

"Trust me to do what?"

He stood and paced the room for a few seconds, seemingly oblivious to Bruce dancing around his feet. "To like me for me," he said softly. "To want me…for me."

Val couldn't believe what she was hearing. Insecurity. Vulnerability. Things she knew a man like Jake would consider a weakness.

"You thought I might only be interested in your bank account, and that's why you didn't tell me who you really were?"

He shrugged, his broad shoulders sagging. "I had to be sure."

Val heard the pain in his words, overwhelmed by the reality of what he was feeling. After Diego, she'd also questioned her worth, and she hadn't experienced anywhere near the betrayal that Jake had. But she still didn't entirely understand his feelings, considering she came from the Fortunado family.

"I never hid who I was from you, Jake," she said quietly. "I might not have been shouting my family tree from the rooftops, but it was never a secret. My family is well off and—"

"In trouble," he added and then shrugged again.

Val's spine straightened. Suddenly she understood

him completely. "You didn't trust me because you believed my family's business is in financial trouble and that somehow I might be a threat to your precious bank balance."

"I couldn't be sure."

Her disbelief turned to anger. "Are you that self-absorbed, Jake?"

"Of course not. I'm not saying this to hurt you, Valene. You wanted the truth," he reminded her. "This is it. I have trust issues, okay? Big trust issues. But I have genuine feelings for you and I don't want to—"

"Genuine feelings?" she echoed. "Yes, I can tell. I can feel every one of those *feelings* each time you insinuate that my family and I are after your money."

"That's not what I said," he remarked, clearly frustrated. "You're mixing up my words. I care about you. I want to pursue our relationship further. I want to date you. I want to make love to you and wake up next to you. I want all those things, Valene. And I'm hoping that we can have them now that we've cleared the air."

"Cleared the air?" She laughed loudly. "Is that what you think? For the record, the air is not cleared. It's about as hazy as it gets. My family doesn't need your money."

He sighed heavily. "I'm not trying to insult your family."

"Maybe you're not, but you're doing a great job, regardless." She checked her watch. "You need to leave now."

He looked skeptical. "Is your date running late?"

"No, I'm sure he'll be on time as always."

She wasn't about to tell him that her parents were picking her up and they were going out to dinner together. Jake had no right to assume anything about her. He'd done enough of that already!

"Please don't go out with another man...not while we're in the middle of this."

Pity for the obvious anguish in his voice quickly took hold of her. "It's not that kind of date. If you must know, I'm meeting my parents for dinner. But I still want you to leave." She gave him the takeout food she'd placed on the counter. "Go home, Jake. I need some time to digest all this information."

"When can I see you again?"

She shrugged. "I'm not sure."

"I don't want this to be the end of us, Valene."

She didn't want that either...not really. But she was hurting through to her bones.

"Good night, Jake."

Once he was gone, Val sagged against the back of the door, propped up on knees she had to lock into place. Damn his gorgeous hide. She shouldn't have let him in. She shouldn't have listened to his explanation. Because now she was more conflicted than she was before.

The problem was, Val was as much in love with Jake Brockton as she'd ever been.

And she was pretty sure he knew it.

Chapter Twelve

Valene didn't hear from Jake for three days. Three of the longest days of her life. She knew he was giving her space, exactly as she'd requested, but she couldn't believe how much she yearned to hear the sound of his voice, or taste his kiss, or feel his breath against her skin.

On Monday he sent her flowers, lots of them—the store-bought variety—which irritated her to no end, even though all the women in the office thought it was hopelessly romantic. On Tuesday it was a stuffed toy in the shape of a bulldog, and Wednesday it was a poster from her favorite zombie television show. Even Maddie sighed a little at his efforts.

"Since when did you become the president of Jake's fan club?" she queried in the lunchroom when her sister asked if she'd seen him.

"I'm not," Maddie replied. "Just wondering how you feel about him at the moment."

"Angry," she replied. "Hurt. Disappointed. He truly thought I would be after his money."

"Well," Maddie said and shrugged, "people are often motivated by a lot less."

Val's gaze narrowed. "What are you suggesting, Maddie, that I simply forgive him and move on?"

"Maybe that's not such a bad idea."

Val stirred extra sugar into her coffee. "I'm not so sure you'd be as forgiving of Zach if you were in my situation."

Maddie rested her hip against the countertop. "Do you remember when Dad pitted Zach and me against one another for the CEO position?"

"Of course."

"Do you remember how I thought Zach had deliberately gone behind my back with a client?"

Val remembered the whole situation. It was the first time she'd witnessed her usually reserved sister at the mercy of her emotions. "I remember."

"And of course, that wasn't the case. But I jumped to conclusions based on the facts I believed I knew."

"It's hardly the same scenario," Val pointed out. "For one, Zach was crazy in love with you."

Maddie's brows rose. "And you don't believe Jake is in love with you?"

"I think he wants me," she admitted, hurting all over. "I think the sex is great and we get along and we became friends and enjoy spending time together and somehow that started to feel like more. But he lied to me, over and over. I believed he was someone else. In all that time when we were getting to know one another, I thought he was a certain kind of man, and he's not. He's rich and successful, and as Dad pointed out, he could buy us out ten times over."

"You almost sound as though you'd prefer he be a penniless ranch hand."

Val sighed. "I'd prefer he was honest from the beginning. I'd prefer that what we had was real and not simply Jake moving me around like a piece on a chessboard. It feels like Diego all over again."

"Except that Jake *isn't* Diego," Maddie reminded her. "He hasn't asked for anything from you other than *you*. What are you so scared of facing, Val?"

"The truth," she said dully. "I was duped. Made to look foolish."

"In whose eyes?"

"Mine," she admitted.

"So, your reaction is about pride?"

Val swallowed the heat in her throat. "It's about value. How I value myself. And that I'm not just *little* Valene, the spoiled daughter of Kenneth Fortunado, who will tolerate anything because I'm compliant and good-natured and easily manipulated. I know I'm not going to change the world, Maddie. I'm not extreme—I'm not passionate about causes like Schuyler is or driven by a need for success like you are. I'm middle-of-the-road. I'm reliable and predictable in the feelings department. I'm the person who always buys an extra gift on the holidays just in case someone unexpected turns up. I'm the person who will always be the designated driver on a night out. I'm the person a gold-digging creep like Diego would target, because I am gullible and have an insatiable need to be liked. I'm the person a man like Hugh would want to be with, because I will never be chaotic or unpredictable."

"And Jake?"

"Honestly," she replied, "I have no idea why Jake is attracted to me."

"Why don't you ask him?"

"I'm not sure I want to hear the answer."

Maddie reached out and unexpectedly hugged her. "You're strong and beautiful and kind, and being around you is like balm for the soul, Val. That's why Jake is attracted to you. It's why we all love you. Why we all need to be around you. You make our lives better. You make the world better."

Val's eyes filled with tears. "I love him, Maddie."

Her sister squeezed her tightly. "I know you do."

"I just don't know if I can forgive him."

"Well, the only way you're going to find out is if you talk to him."

Val knew Maddie was right. When she returned to her office, she stared at the flowers for a few minutes. It took about an hour of emotional yo-yoing before she garnered the courage to grab her phone.

I think we should talk. V.

The text reply came back in about ten seconds.

Love to. Tell me when. J.

She took a breath and sent another message.

Coffee. Tomorrow. Eleven. You know the place. V.

He replied with a thumbs-up emoji. They had a date. It would be make or break. Being in love with Jake was one thing—it was out of her control—but forgiveness was harder. Because if she did forgive him for deceiving her, she'd open herself up to vulnerability and potential heartbreak. It was a giant leap for Val.

Being with Diego, and even Hugh, had switched off something inside her. Diego had used her. Hugh had admitted he didn't love her but she was suitable wife material. She thought about Jake's words about being wanted for *who* he was, not his bank balance, and Val understood. Neither of her previous relationships had been about her. For Diego, it was the money, for Hugh, her family tree. The realization had left her with envy in her heart when her two sisters had found love. Not jealousy—because she wasn't that mean-spirited and she truly adored both Maddie and Schuyler—but she knew she wanted the same kind of deep connection with someone. The way Zach adored Maddie, the way he relaxed her often prickly defenses through love and commitment and support. And the way Carlo clearly loved Schuyler more than life itself, revering her craziness, keeping her grounded. It's why she'd logged on to the dating app. Why she'd punched in her details and opened herself up to the possibility of meeting a man that a computer program insisted was her perfect match.

And she'd met him.

Hardworking, successful, strong, funny, a man who possessed a strict moral compass. A man who cared for the people around him, who'd quit college to protect his family, who'd built a business from the ground up using sweat and smarts and steely determination.

Too bad he'd also deceived her like the lousy rat he was.

When Val walked into the coffeehouse the following morning, she realized she was more nervous than when she'd done the same thing a month earlier.

A lot had happened since then.

The place was empty except for someone ordering at the counter and a young couple sitting at a table in the back. Val looked around, seeing no sign of Jake, and walked toward the same booth where they'd sat on their first meeting.

A few minutes later, Jake strode through the doors. He looked so gorgeous, so tall and broad and familiar. He spotted her immediately and headed for the booth.

"Mornin'," he said and sat down.

A waiter approached and took their order, and once the young man left, Val spoke.

"Thank you for meeting me."

He met her gaze. "It's good to see you. How are you?"

"Okay. You?"

"Better for seeing you," he said candidly. "I have some news from the shelter. It looks as though Digby will get his own family."

Val's heart rolled over. "I'm so glad."

"See, sometimes everyone does get their happily-ever-after."

She placed her hands on the table. "Thank you for the zombie poster."

He grinned. "My pleasure."

"The flowers and stuffed toy were a bit over-the-top."

He shrugged. "I just want to make sure you keep thinking about me."

Val made a face. "I don't think I could stop thinking about you even if I tried. But I'm still mad at you."

"I know."

"However, I'm trying to be a grown-up about it," she admitted. "I'm trying to keep things in perspective."

"Like how?"

"Like, I know you didn't tell me who you were because you didn't want to be judged...but by not telling me, you were judging *me*. And my family. Something I take very personally."

"I'm sorry I hurt you, Valene."

Val heard the earnestness in his voice, took a breath and was about to speak when they were interrupted by the waiter with their coffees. After he left, she said, "Okay, let's take a small step and have a do-over."

"A do-over?"

"Yes." She held out her hand. "Hi, my name is Valene Fortunado. I'm twenty-four, single, I work in my family's business, where things have been a little tough recently. I live in a condo my father bought for me, I have a dog called Bruce, and I once paid twelve hundred dollars for a pair of shoes. I'm spoiled and have an opinion about pretty much everything."

He grinned as he shook her hand. "I'm Jake Brockton. Thirty-two, divorced, with major trust issues. I own a very successful ranch outside Fulshear and worry that I'm going to be wanted for my money and not myself."

"See," Val said with a fake smile. "That wasn't so difficult, was it?"

"Harder than you can possibly imagine."

"Don't keep things from me again, Jake. Trust goes both ways."

"I know," he said quietly. "I'm learning to let go of the past, Valene."

She nodded. "I understand. All my life I've been overprotected and looked after. It's as though my family doesn't believe I can handle the hard stuff. But I can," she assured him. "I can handle whatever I need to. I can fight fires and slay dragons—and of course I don't mean that in the literal sense, but you get the drift. I know my parents treat me differently because I'm the youngest, and in many ways, I appreciate being shielded from the world…but sometimes I wish everyone in my family would treat me as though I am a grown-up and able to fully contribute in a meaningful way."

"You think they don't?"

"I think I got the job at Fortunado Real Estate as a way of keeping me close. My parents were worried that I was planning on going to college out of state—which was never the case. I love Houston and I love being close to my family. But still, sometimes I'm smothered by their need to keep a watchful eye on everything I do."

"Family is all that matters, Valene, and if they smother you, it's only because they care."

"That's a nice sentiment, Jake, but I wouldn't expect a self-made man to understand." She laughed humorlessly. "You know, the irony is, my father would really like you."

"I'd like to meet him. And your mom."

Val took a breath. "Okay. Friday night. My parents are having a family get-together. Schuyler and Carlo are driving in from Austin, and my brother Everett and his wife, Lila, will be there—I think I told you that he's a doctor. And my other brother Gavin and his fiancée, who I haven't seen since Maddie's wedding last month. He's a workaholic lawyer. Plus Maddie and Zach."

"Will I be there as your date?"

"I haven't decided," she replied. "To be honest, I haven't decided if I'll forgive you, either."

He leaned forward and rested his elbows on the table. "I think for both our sakes you should. You know, I haven't forgotten what you said to me at the ranch last week."

Val knew immediately what he was referring to. "That was a heat-of-the-moment thing. I was angry and worked up and I can't be blamed for things that might have been said rashly and without proper consideration."

He laughed. "Have you been practicing that perfectly eloquent backpedal, Valene?"

Val's skin heated. "You're such a horse's ass, Jake. I'm not going to incriminate myself any further. Are you accepting the invitation to meet my parents or not?"

"Of course."

Val drank her latte and then wiggled a little in the booth, indicating she was ready to leave. "I'll text you my parents' home address."

"I'll pick you up and we'll go together."

She wasn't about to let him have his own way. "That's the offer, Jake. Meet me there or don't show."

His mouth flattened. "Okay, I accept your terms."

She nodded. "See you Friday. Seven o'clock."

And then she left as swiftly as her legs allowed.

The Fortunado estate is impressive, Jake thought as he pulled in the driveway. He spotted Val's Lexus immediately and parked the Sierra behind a white Volvo and a red BMW. He got out, strode onto the wide front porch and then knocked on the huge wooden double doors. A few minutes later, the door opened and a middle-aged woman appeared. She was tall and attractive, and he recognized Valene's brown eyes.

"You must be Jake," she said, her voice soft and cultured and *very* southern. "I'm Barbara Fortunado. It's lovely to meet you."

Jake shook her hand and was politely ushered inside. The house, as expected, was well appointed and tasteful, and the floors gleamed with polish. "Thank you for inviting me."

Barbara smiled. "My daughter is quite taken with you."

Jake chuckled. "Yeah, but I don't think she likes me very much at the moment."

"She's stubborn," the older woman said quietly. "She gets that from her father. She's also unwaveringly honest. She gets that from me. We've spoiled her, of course, but I imagine you know that. That being said, she has such a kind and forgiving heart, I don't imagine she will stay angry with you forever."

He grinned. "I hope not."

"For the record, when one of my cubs is hurting, I do tend to get a little lioness about things."

"Oh, God, Mom, let him at least get in the house before you start giving him the talk."

Jake heard Valene's voice and then spotted her when she appeared in the hallway, her heels clicking over the floorboards. Bruce was bounding behind her, followed by a fluff ball that he suspected was Maddie's pet, Ramona. Valene had told him all about her sister's very pampered pooch the day they'd spent volunteering at the animal shelter.

He met Valene's gaze, wanting desperately to haul her into his arms and kiss her. But he didn't. For one thing, Barbara Fortunado was watching them keenly, and for another, he was certain Valene would take a swing at him if he tried.

"Valene has told me about the good work you're doing with the Fortunado Foundation," he told her mother. "I'd like to talk with you about it sometime."

"You're interested in charity work?"

He nodded. "I'm interested in learning more about your foundation. I support a few local charitable organizations, but if I can help with your charity, I will."

Valene was frowning. "Yes, Mom, he is perfectly serious. Jake's a born do-gooder. You two will get along famously."

He passed Valene the two bottles of wine he'd brought, and she grabbed his arm. She looked so good, so sexy in a short red tunic dress and black boots.

"Cute outfit."

She gave a wide smile. "You don't look so bad yourself."

He glanced down, pleased he'd ditched his usual jeans and Western shirt for taupe cargos, a white shirt and a leather aviator-style jacket. "I can tone down the cowboy thing every now and then."

"So I see," she said and moved closer, leading him into the kitchen. "But you know, I've kinda gotten used to that cowboy thing you've got going."

Before he could reply, the room erupted in a series of greetings and introductions. Kenneth Fortunado was naturally reserved at first, but the rest of her family was friendly and talkative. Her brother Everett and his wife, Lila, were nice people, as were Gavin and his fiancée, and Maddie surprisingly kissed his cheek.

Before dinner, Kenneth cornered him, but Jake didn't mind. He figured he'd be equally suspicious if he had a daughter. Which only made him imagine what it would be like to have a child with Valene. Which was, he realized, something he genuinely wanted.

"My daughter spoke very highly of you," the older man said.

Spoke. Past tense. "She's quite a woman."

Kenneth nodded. "Of course, she told you I had an investigator check out your history. I had to, you understand, as there have been attempts to sabotage my business, and with everything that is going on with the

Robinson family and the Fortunes—" He paused. "I suppose you know about that, too?"

"Valene mentioned it."

"If I had my way, I would forget the Fortunes exist, particularly the fact that I'm related to them. But I have to protect my family."

"I understand," Jake replied, trying not to feel too outraged at the blatant invasion of his privacy. "I trust Valene has explained to you some of the details of my divorce?"

"She said enough," Kenneth replied. "She's still very upset with you for deceiving her."

"I know," Jake said as he caught her laughter from the other side of the room.

"My wife and I have overprotected her," Kenneth admitted. "Naturally, with the last child, you try to learn from the mistakes you made with the others. Not that she needed it. But we indulged her and tried to make things as easy as possible for her. But she's stubborn—she gets that from her mother," he said and grinned. "Anyway, I wanted to apologize for digging into your past."

Jake wondered if Kenneth would have been less apologetic had he not discovered Jake's net worth, but he shrugged off the thought. He didn't want to resent Valene's family, and he was genuinely interested in helping the Fortunado Foundation, about which he'd heard great things. It was time he got back to living a full life and started doing things that were important to him. His work at the shelter was important, but with his resources, Jake knew he could do so much more.

"No sweat," he said and smiled. "Are you any closer to finding out who is behind all of the trouble?"

Kenneth shrugged. "Not yet. But I know one thing— there are a few too many coincidences for it to be mere chance. And I'll tell you, when I find the person or persons responsible, they will regret the day they took on my family and expected to win."

"Well, if you need someone in your corner, let me know."

"Thank you, son, that's very generous."

Dinner was served in the dining room, a delicious meal of selected meats and vegetables. Valene was on one side of him, Barbara Fortunado on the other, and he was complimenting the chef when Schuyler Mendoza spoke.

"So, you're, like, some kind of mega-rich beef magnate?" she asked Jake.

Jake felt Valene's arm press against his, and since it was the most intimate contact they'd had in weeks, he didn't flinch. "Something like that."

"You're well off the social media grid. I'm not sure how you've managed to do that."

He wasn't about to admit that he'd avoided all social media since his divorce because he knew Patrice would try to keep track of his movements.

"I don't do the selfie thing."

Valene's brothers groaned in agreement, and Schuyler shrugged when Valene made a protesting sound. "Well, of course I tried to find out what I could about you, since my sister has old-fashioned ideas about a person's right to privacy and all that."

Jake pushed back in his chair, aware that everyone at the table was waiting for his response. But Valene had told him enough about her beloved sister to know the other woman was simply good-natured and nosy. Even though her husband was giving her a cautious glance.

"What would you like to know?" he inquired.

Both her brows rose high. "How old were you when you made your first million?"

"Twenty-six."

"How much are you worth now?" she asked.

"A lot."

Everyone laughed, and Jake did his best to keep a straight face. Only Valene looked outraged. He touched her hand reassuringly, making it clear he was very capable of handling a few inappropriate questions.

"Really, Sky, is this necessary?" Valene demanded.

"No," her sister replied. "But I've got a curious nature. What else do you do besides sell really expensive steaks?"

Jake smiled. "I donate to charity. I invest in some property development. I buy overpriced horses. I'm currently renovating my home. Anything else?"

The mood shifted, laughter rang around the table and he urged Valene to relax once everyone continued eating their meals.

"Stop being such a worrier," he said softly so only she could hear.

"I'm sorry Schuyler is such a pain. She doesn't have a filter and thinks that—"

"Wait until you meet my sister," he said, cutting her off. "She's the pain of the century."

"I'd like to meet her."

"I'm sure she'd like that, too."

"Jake." Gavin Fortunado said his name and diverted his attention from Valene for a moment. "I believe you know a client of mine. He mentioned you the other day. Karl Messer? From the Messer Group? He does those high-rises and shopping malls."

Jake's back straightened, because even though people around him continued to chatter, Valene was suddenly as still as a statue. He looked directly at Gavin as he replied. "We went to school together."

"You know Karl Messer?"

Valene's voice was ice-cold.

"Yes."

He watched as her throat rolled convulsively. "Are you one of his silent investors?"

"At times."

She jumped to the obvious and correct conclusion. "Are you the reason he called me?"

Jake knew there was no getting away from the truth. "I gave him your number."

She was on her feet in a microsecond, tossing her napkin on the table. "I've lost my appetite."

She stormed off, leaving everyone at the table sitting in stunned silence. Until Schuyler spoke again.

"Um, what just happened?"

Maddie sighed heavily, Kenneth was shaking his head and Zach shrugged.

"I should go to her," Maddie said and started to get up.

Jake stood immediately and held out a hand. "It's my medicine," he said as he pushed the chair in. "I'll take it."

He left the room and headed for the kitchen. Valene was by the sink, a glass of cold water pressed against her temple, her eyes closed. But she clearly sensed his presence, because she spoke first.

"I don't want to talk to you."

"I'm pretty sure you do," he said and moved around the counter. "Because I know you want an explanation."

She harrumphed. "Oh, I think I can figure this one out for myself. You called your old school buddy Karl and asked him to help me out because I'm such an utter failure at what I do and clearly unable to do my job without interference from my knight in shining armor.

Does that about cover it?" she asked him, opening her eyes and spearing him with a look.

"I gave him your number," Jake insisted, "and that's all. Any business agreements that were made between the Messer Group and Fortunado Real Estate were made because of you, not me."

She didn't look convinced. "You gave him my number? You asked him to call me. *Told* him, is probably more to the point. Do you think I can't read between the lines here, Jake?"

"Read what?" he shot back. "Karl and I went to school together. We sometimes do business together. He's a trustworthy and successful operator. Having him as an exclusive client will be good for your business."

"And good for *me*, right?"

Jake sighed, exasperated. "Why are you getting so worked up?"

"Why?" she shot back. "Because I don't need help to be successful. I don't need to be spoon-fed to do my job."

"That's hardly what I did."

She was glaring, her beautiful cheeks scorched with color. "What about Otis McAvoy? Did you send him to me, too?"

Jake nodded. "He was a friend of my dad's."

"Ha," she said sarcastically. "I guess I need to screen every single client I've taken on in the last month to make sure they weren't setups by my stupid, thoughtless, controlling, multimillionaire boyfriend!"

Jake rocked back on his heels. "At least you're calling me your boyfriend."

She glared at him, her hands on her hips. "Is that all you got from that? Can you not see why I'm so angry?"

"I know why, but I think you're overreacting."

She moved around the marble island, her chest heaving. "I guess you would. That's the standard reply from a control freak."

"I'm not a control freak, Valene. I saw that you were in trouble and wanted to help you."

"I don't need help. Don't you get it, Jake? For the first time in my life, I actually believed I had done something on my own, without my father or my family making things easier. But it was just a lie," she said quietly. "Like everything with you."

Jake sighed heavily. "Valene, this is just your pride talking. If you take some time and think about—"

"This isn't pride," she insisted. "It's respect. Self-respect. I don't want to be another notch on your charity bedpost, Jake. I'm not like one of those homeless puppies at the animal shelter who need you to fix things. I don't need fixing. Like you, I want to make my own way in the world. I want to be successful and make a difference. But I won't do that on the coattails of someone else's influence."

She inhaled deeply, and Jake noticed how much her hands were shaking. He desperately wanted to take her into his arms, to make her see sense, to show her that anything he did, he did because he cared about her.

"My intention wasn't to—"

"Your intention," she said hotly, cutting him off, "is to get whatever you want, in whatever way you can get it. I've been around men like you all my life. Money and success is a breeding ground for that kind of arrogance. But I don't want to be a part of that environment. I never have. Perhaps that's why I'm below par in the successful career department. Why I'm mediocre at best at what I do."

Jake couldn't believe what he was hearing. "You're not mediocre, Valene."

"No? I guess I'll never know, since everyone around me thinks I need propping up. Well," she said, laughing humorlessly, "I'm over being treated like the weak link. I guess in a way I should thank you. If it wasn't for you, Jake, I might have continued to walk in the shadow of everyone around me for the rest of my life."

He frowned. "What does that mean?"

"It means that we're done," she said and walked past him. Jake followed her back down the hallway and into the dining room. He noticed the startled expressions on the faces of everyone in the room. And Valene— vibrant and passionate and unbelievably sexy as she strode around the table, her shoulders back, her chin held at a defiant tilt—wasn't finished yet.

"Dad, Maddie, Zach," she said and took a deep breath. "I quit!"

Chapter Thirteen

It was day five of #CowboyGate, and the Fortunado Real Estate office was still in a kind of vibrating shock.

Val had dropped her resignation letter on Maddie's desk first thing Monday morning, before she'd headed to Austin to meet with a client and also to cool off for a day or so. Now it was Wednesday and she was back in Houston.

And the place was still in an uproar.

But she held her resolve. Val had no intention of being swayed from her decision. She was about to embark on a new and totally independent phase in her life and wasn't allowing anyone to change her mind.

Of course, "anyone" hadn't made contact.

Jake had been unusually quiet since the drama that had ensued at her parents' home the previous Friday. Naturally, her family all thought he was quite wonderful. Both Schuyler and her mother thought he was Mr. Romance of the Century, Maddie told her she was overreacting, Gavin said he shouldn't have made any comment about Karl Messer, and her father told her not to be hasty. But Val wasn't backing down. Jake had gone too far. She wasn't anyone's charity case, particularly for a tall, good-looking cowboy who believed he owned enough of the world to ensnare her in his web of deceit and lies and manipulation.

Yep, she had made the right decision calling things off.

It wasn't as though she still loved him or anything.

It had been a passing phase. Just sexual chemistry. She had been in love with the idea of being in love. And now she was completely over her fleeting infatuation. Besides, the lying, underhanded rat didn't deserve her.

Val got up from her desk and headed from the office, making her way down the hall to Maddie's much larger office that overlooked the street. Her sister was on the phone, but she beckoned her into the room the moment she spotted her in the doorway. She ended the call and gave Val her complete attention.

"Hey, Val, what's up?"

Of course, everyone was being extra nice to her, extra sensitive, extra understanding.

"I sent through the Messer file to your email. You can decide what you want to do with it."

Maddie sighed. "You're sure that's what you want, Val?"

"Positive." She lingered for a moment. "And the McAvoy account is on Zach's desk. Where is Zach, anyway? I've called him twice this morning. And his office door is closed."

"He's in a meeting with a client."

Val nodded. Zach rarely took meetings behind closed doors. "Important client, huh?"

"You could say that. I'm just heading there now. So…

you're sure you want to quit?" she queried as she got to her feet. "Seems like you're still interested in what's going on around here."

"You have my notice," she replied. "And I'll continue to work up until my last day, which is next Friday."

"And then what?"

She shrugged. "I haven't completely decided. I have some money saved, so I thought I'd take a sabbatical and do some charity work."

"I'm sure Mom would find a place for you at the Fortunado Foundation, if that's what you want."

Val's spine straightened. "Oh, you mean take another family handout because I'm too incompetent to make it on my own?"

"That's not what I mean."

Val shrugged, tired of the conversation, tired of everyone thinking they knew what was best for her. "I'm going to sort through my client list today and make sure everything is up-to-date. I'll be in my office if you need me."

She headed back down the hall and slumped in her chair. She pulled up her client listing on her laptop, made a few notes, then got into the folder she kept for Maddie's clients who overlapped with her own and almost reeled back when she saw a file named Brockton. Of course it was password protected, but that didn't stop Val's imagination from surging into overdrive. She raced from the room and headed to Maddie's office. She walked around her sister's desk and stared at the open day planner. For all Maddie's ability to embrace technology, her uptight sister still preferred an old-fashioned way of diarizing her appointments. And there, on today's docket, she saw it in black and white.

Jake Brockton. Eleven o'clock.

Anger surged through her blood.

She strode out of the room and headed to Zach's office, the room next to Maddie's. She knocked and then opened the door, not waiting for an invitation to enter.

And then she stared, long and hard, at the three people sitting around the huge desk.

Her sister. Her brother-in-law. And her former lover. Former friend. Former *everything*.

"Val?" Maddie's voice sounded higher-pitched than usual.

"What's going on?" she demanded, hands on hips, so fired up she thought she was going to bust a blood vessel.

"Valene," Jake said, on his feet in a second and taking a step toward her. "I can explain."

Val glared at him and ignored the two other people in the room. "Why is there a client file with your name on it? And why are you in a meeting with the CEOs of this company? The company my father started. The company I've worked for."

"It's business."

"Funny business," she shot back with a brittle laugh.

"I've been planning to expand the business into Austin for some time, so Maddie and Zach are looking for potential sites in that area. There's nothing sinister going on, Valene."

It sounded simple and logical. She looked at her sister. "And you think, despite the situation, it's acceptable to do this?"

"It's business, like Jake said," Maddie replied.

She turned her attention back to Jake. "And this is the only real estate agency in Houston that can assist in this sudden grand plan you have to carve out a beef empire?" she asked sarcastically, refusing to think about how gorgeous he looked in his regulation jeans, Western shirt and dark jacket. She'd missed him so much. More than she'd believed she could miss anyone. She missed his nightly phone calls, his silly jokes, his willingness to watch zombie flicks even though she knew he didn't like them. And she missed his arms around her. So much.

"Of course not, but Fortunado is the best, correct?"

He was right, but Val wasn't convinced of his motives. In fact, she knew exactly what he was doing. And what Maddie and Zach were up to. Since the family had discovered that Jake was dipped in gold, they'd spent hours talking about him, so she wasn't convinced of the purity of their motives, either. In fact, the whole situation reeked of manipulation and greed. And she wasn't sure whom she was madder at in that moment—Jake or Maddie and Zach.

"It's not enough that you threw Messer and McAvoy in my path?" she demanded. "Now this?"

"I was trying to help you."

"That's exactly my point," she said hotly. "I don't need anyone's help. And it's not your place to help me."

His head tilted fractionally. "Are you sure about that?"

"I'm *sure* that you don't have the right to run interference just because we've had sex a few times."

Maddie gasped, clearly uncomfortable by the tone of the conversation. "Maybe Zach and I should leave you both alone and—"

"Don't bother," Val snapped. "*I'm* leaving."

"Avoiding this, or me," Jake said quietly, "isn't going to make the situation go away, Valene."

"Want to bet?" She laughed humorlessly. "Keep in mind that we wouldn't have a situation if you hadn't lied your ass off when we first met, or you hadn't gotten your friends to take pity and make me look good in my job, or if my *bosses* hadn't suddenly decided to help you expand your empire. Cut the crap, Jake. This is about one thing. You did all this because of me."

"Well, of course it's because of you!" he said, clearly exasperated.

Val rolled back on her heels. "But…why?"

He stared at her, his glittering blue eyes unwavering in their intensity. "Why do you think?"

She swallowed hard, unsure of what she saw in his expression. "Because…because you want to control me and—"

"If you could look past your pride for one minute," he said quietly, cutting her off, his breath heavy, "you'd know why. I don't want to control you, Valene. Frankly, that would be like trying to hold back the tide. But ask yourself why you're so determined to think the worst of me, and why things changed the moment you found out I *wasn't* that working-class ranch hand you seemed to like so much. You want to talk about control?" he said. "Think about that!"

He left then, striding from the room with a brief farewell to Zach and Maddie and saying nothing more to her. Once he was out of sight, Val slumped back against one of the office chairs.

"Val," Maddie said softly. "Go after him."

She shook her head, hurting all over. "Why would you both think it's okay to be in business with him? Why did you approach him? Why did you—"

"We didn't," Zach explained. "He approached us."

That didn't make her feel any better. "And you both thought it would be okay to take advantage of his… of his…"

"Of his feelings for you?" Maddie offered, regarding her gently.

His feelings…

Val had been so wound up, so angry, so vehement and hurt she hadn't spent a second considering he had a motive other than his need to control her. "I'm not sure he has—"

"Val," Zach said with an impatient groan, "for pity's sake, the guy is obviously crazy in love with you."

Her heart almost stopped. Could that be true? Of course, she knew he cared. And she knew they had chemistry and an amazing connection unlike any she'd known before. But love? When she'd blurted out her own feelings weeks earlier, he hadn't responded, hadn't said anything. Sure, he'd still pursued her...but love?

"Even if he does...feel...you know, whatever," she said, stumbling over her words as heat suffused her cheeks, "that doesn't give you the right to use that to the advantage of the business. We don't operate that way, and I have always believed that both of you had more scruples. And I won't have anyone using me as a pawn or a reason to fleece him."

Maddie clapped her hands, smiling broadly. "It's good to see you fighting for what you want, Val. But honestly, I don't think anyone could take advantage of Jake. He's very much his own man. The only person who has that kind of influence is you. And he's right in what he said," Maddie reminded her. "Ever since you found out he was wealthy, you have backed off and looked for reasons to end your relationship. Which, logically, makes no sense. You said you wanted someone who ticked all your boxes. Well, kiddo, he does. And that terrifies you. He's not after your connections like Diego, and he's not after a compliant and suitable match like Hugh. But you're still cautious, and there's a reason for that. Maybe it's time to face what that is?"

Val stared at her sister, dumbstruck. Because Maddie's point was irrefutable. She had fallen for Jake when she believed he was exactly the opposite of what she wanted. And she'd hidden behind her outrage at his deception as a shield against the real issue: she was terrified he would really see her. Every flaw. Every failing. Her lack of real ambition. Her average grades in school and college. Her constant fear that she wasn't reaching her potential, that she was one of the *lesser* Fortunados. And that what she really wanted—to find a man who loved her, to raise a family, to nurture—would be seen as an easy out, settling, taking the uncomplicated route.

But what Val really wanted, what she yearned for, was a family of her own.

She'd never been motivated by ambition or money or kudos. But she was a Fortunado, and there were expectations. Perhaps if she'd been a free spirit like Schuyler, creative and energetic in her approach to life, she might have been given a free pass. But she was Valene—the youngest—the girl who was the apple of her parents' eyes and could do no wrong. So, she did no wrong. She went to school, college, began working at Fortunado Real Estate. For a while she'd even dated a man handpicked by her father, because after the disaster with Diego, it was obvious she couldn't choose someone herself.

And then there was Jake.

Handsome and hardworking. A man who knew who he was. A man who she believed didn't tick any of her boxes—and yet, she was drawn to him unlike she'd ever been to anyone before. And with him, she didn't have to be Valene Fortunado—she could be Val, exactly who *she* was. No expectations. No judgment. Because she'd believed he was also unambitious and happy to live his life in the present. And he was right…she had judged him. She had all the control while she believed he was a penniless ranch hand. In retrospect, she'd been arrogant and haughty and completely self-obsessed. Everything she despised.

She was ashamed of herself. Of her condemnation. Of her blatant condescension, her self-serving superiority. It was a wonder he hadn't run a mile in the opposite direction the moment she'd raised a brow at his crappy old truck or asked him if he owned a suit. And she'd stayed angry at him for weeks because she was trapped by her own egotistical pride. When the truth was, she loved him. She loved everything about him. And she wanted to spend the rest of her life showing him how much.

She just hoped it wasn't too late.

On Sunday afternoon, Jake was finally able to pull the covers off all the furniture in the ranch house. It had been a long time since the place had been dusted or cleaned, and as he piled up the covers in the downstairs living room, he realized he needed to give the place a thorough going-over. He'd slept in the house for the past three nights, having replaced the furniture in the upstairs bedroom. The work, he figured, would do him some good. It would exorcize his demons and maybe help alleviate the constant ache in his heart.

"Is that the last of them?"

He looked up as his mom walked in from the kitchen. "Yep."

She glanced around. "You need some new furniture."

It was true. There were several empty spaces around the room, including where the antique armoire had been, and the matching dining table and chairs. Patrice had taken them, along with most of the other antiquities he'd sourced over the years.

"I think I might ditch all of this stuff," he said, looking around at the pieces that were left, some of them worth a small fortune. Patrice had liked antiques, but Jake wanted to add some more modern furniture into the place. "Maybe we'll have a yard sale."

She crossed her arms. "Great idea."

"You know," he said and tossed the stack of covers into a box, "you can move in here if you want. There's plenty of room."

"And cramp your style?" she queried and smiled. "No, I'm very happy in my little cottage out in the back. This is a house that needs to have a family in it—a mom, a dad and a whole bunch of kids. A family you need to make, son."

Jake shoved the lid down on the box. "Not much chance of that," he muttered.

His mother sighed. "Well, have you called her?"

No...

But he missed her. He wasn't sure how he would stop missing her.

"She made her opinion very clear, Mom," he said as he closed up another box.

"She's upset," Lynda said quietly. "Naturally so. But you should talk to her, try to work things out."

He wanted to. But he didn't want to get another dose of her rejection. He was still stinging, still hurting, still trying to figure out what he could have done differently.

Everything...

He should have been up front from the beginning. He should have told her who and what he was. And he sure as hell shouldn't have started interfering in her work. He'd gotten, he figured, exactly what he deserved. But even knowing he'd behaved like a jackass, he still couldn't believe she wouldn't see the real reason behind his behavior. That's what tortured him, that she didn't understand. He'd believed she knew him better. But he'd been wrong. While Jake had fallen headlong and crazy in love with her, it was obvious that Valene had only been in love with the idea of being in love. And *that* couldn't last. Still, part of him wanted to believe that her feelings were real and as intense as his own. He remembered how she'd cursed at him for making her fall in love with him, as though it was the last thing she wanted, and then backpedaled when he called her out on it.

Beside him, Sheba gave a loud bark, and he heard a vehicle pull up outside. "Someone's here," he said, ending the conversation with his mother. Jake grabbed the box and headed for the door, crossing the threshold before he came to an abrupt halt.

Valene stood at the bottom of the steps. Dressed in jeans, high boots, a black sweater and a long white woolen coat, she looked more beautiful than he had ever seen her. Her hair was loose, framing her face, and since it was a chilly afternoon, her cheeks and nose were rosy.

He dropped the box as Sheba raced down the steps to greet her. He watched, aching inside, as she bent down to pet the dog and then straightened. "Hi," she said softly, placing a foot on the bottom step.

"Hello."

He heard his mother shuffling behind him. "I'll make myself scarce," she said discreetly, quickly moving down the steps and grabbing Sheba's collar. "I'll take her with me. It's good to see you, Val," his mom said and then hurriedly took the path leading to the cottage.

"Can we talk?"

Jake pulled himself from his trance and quickly beckoned her inside. "Of course, come on in out of the cold."

She took the steps wordlessly and entered the house,

walking down the hall and into the living room. She took off her jacket and draped it over a chair and stood by the fireplace, then she turned. "You've finished renovating?"

He nodded. "I need to clean up and refurnish the place now."

She looked around. "It's such a lovely house, Jake."

"It's big," he said quietly. "I mean, for one person."

She met his gaze for a second, then looked away. "I thought perhaps your mom and sister might—"

"Mom says she's happy in the cottage," he said, cutting her off. "And Cassidy only comes back every month or so. Besides, it's the kind of house that should have a family in it. You know, kids…"

She traced her hand along the mantel. "Do you…is that what you want?" she asked.

"What I want," he said, taking a breath, "is for you to look at me."

She slowly met his gaze again. Her eyes glistened, and Jake fought every instinct he possessed to not stride across the room and take her into his arms. She looked lost. And hurt. And incredibly vulnerable.

"Why are you here?"

"I didn't… I didn't tell you my whole story," she said raggedly, swallowing hard. "Do you remember our first date when I introduced myself? I didn't tell you everything. I didn't tell you that I worked in my family's business but I was never really happy doing it. I didn't tell you that I've never been very ambitious. I didn't tell you that I had to work extra hard in school to get respectable grades because it's what my parents expected of me. I didn't tell you that I hate my condo but couldn't say that because my father bought it for me, and that's why I got Bruce, because I feel so incredibly alone there. I didn't tell you that when I found out my ex-boyfriend was only interested in me because he wanted a job at Fortunado and I confronted him about it, he called me weak and dull and said I would never amount to anything. And I believed him," she admitted, tears in her eyes. "That's why I dated Hugh. Because he knew what I was and didn't care. Which was worse, in a way, because he was indifferent, and that became a daily reminder of my shortcomings."

Jake's chest ached hearing her admission. "You don't have any shortcomings. You're quite extraordinary."

She stared at him, the tears now on her cheeks, and she managed a small smile.

"Jake..." Her words trailed off. "I'm in love with you."

The ache in his chest vanished, replaced by a tight swell of emotion that sucked the air from his lungs. But he needed to know for certain. "Valene, are you sure you're not simply in love with the idea of being in love?" he asked softly.

"Positive," she replied. "And anyway, I told you I loved you the last time I was here."

"I know you did," he said and took three strides toward her. "I just didn't dare let myself really believe it."

"Believe it," she insisted and laughed through her tears. "But, Jake...are you...are you..."

"Am I what?" he queried, taking her hands gently in his. "Am I in love with you?" He pulled her close. "I am so madly and completely in love with you, Valene, I can barely draw a breath when we're this close."

He kissed her hotly, and she clung to him, her wet cheeks touching his, her mouth exquisitely sweet beneath his. He kissed her again. And again. And she kissed him back, her hands on his shoulders, her soft sighs echoing around the room.

"Are you really sure, Valene?" he whispered against her mouth. "Are you positive it's enough, and not—"

"It's more," she assured him. "I love you, Jake. I love you even if you *are* rich."

He laughed, and it felt so good. "Ah, sweetheart, I'm sorry, you know," he said and dragged her toward the chaise by the window. He sat down and urged her beside him. "I never meant to keep so many secrets, but I had to know. I had to be sure that any feelings you had were for me and not anything else. My ex-wife hammered me, and I—"

She shushed him and placed her fingertips against his mouth. "I know what she did. I know she hurt you and betrayed you. I know she couldn't value what she had, and it made you wary of getting close to anyone. I get it," she said and made a self-deprecating sound. "I understand. And I know it took courage for you to let me into your life," she said and touched his chest. "And into your heart. I love who I am when I'm with you. And I want to spend as much time with you as I can."

Jake grasped her hands. "I don't ever want to be away from you again. And I'm sorry, Valene, about Messer and the whole—"

"We don't have to talk about that," she said quickly.

"Yes, we do," he replied. "Anything I did wasn't done to undermine you or manipulate you. I honestly wanted to help you. And Messer knows good business. I simply pointed him in your direction. You did the rest. The same with Otis. If I overstepped, I apologize. I saw you were hurting, and that your family was in trouble, and it pushed at my overprotective side. If I embarrassed you, I'm sorry. It won't happen again."

"I'm pretty sure it will," she teased and pressed closer. "Let's face it, Jake, you're a good guy. You like helping people, like you did when your dad passed away and you came home so your mom and sister could still live here.

That part of you. That generous, protective side is one of the things I love about you." She sighed and smiled. "I'm not going to pick and choose parts of you to love. I love all of you. I won't pretend I wasn't shocked to learn about your wealth and owning this place and your apparent plans to expand your empire...but I love that you're not obsessed by it."

"I'm not," he said and then chuckled. "Don't get me wrong, I like that I can support the people I care about, and I try to do some good in the community, but the money isn't why I work."

"But," she said, "I don't want you to think you have to *fix* everything."

"Everything?"

"Like my family's business," she replied. "I do know you were trying to help, but I don't want anyone taking advantage of that, either. Particularly Maddie and Zach. If they start bombarding you with business opportunities, they'll have to deal with me."

He chuckled. "My fearless love," he said, loving that she would go to bat to protect him. "But stop fretting. I've planned on expanding the business into other places for a couple of years. But from here on out I will run everything by you beforehand, okay, sweetheart?"

She sighed. "I know Maddie and Zach are worried. And I know my dad said they were getting closer to finding out who is responsible, but I won't allow anyone to manipulate the situation because we fell in love."

He kissed her again, and they stayed on the chaise for a while, making out, holding one another, and then he took her upstairs to his bedroom.

"You got a new bed?" she said when they walked through the doorway.

"I did," he replied. "The old one had too many memories attached to it."

"I'm sorry she hurt you, Jake."

"You know something, I think it stopped hurting the day I met you."

She smiled. "Do you know when I fell in love with you? That day at the animal shelter."

"It took you that long?" he teased. "I knew the moment you ordered that low-fat, single-shot vanilla soy latte with extra cinnamon. And I thought, my God, she's so beautiful, I hope she stays, I hope she likes me, I hope I find out that she wants what I want—marriage, children, family."

She laughed delightfully. "She does. *I do*, Jake. It's all I want. I want to get married one day and make babies with you."

Jake took her hand. "So, once I ask your dad's permission, you'll let me ask you to marry me?"

"Yes, absolutely."

He groaned and led her to the bed. They undressed and then made love slowly, taking time to reacquaint themselves with one another. Jake had never experienced such intense release, such a soul-deep connection to anyone.

Afterward, they lay together, side by side, talking, touching.

"So, are you still intent on leaving Fortunado Real Estate?" he asked, gently stroking her cheek.

She nodded. "I want my work to have value. I want to make a difference."

"Have you given any thought to working at the Fortunado Foundation?

She sighed. "Maddie suggested it. But I'm worried that people might think I –"

"It's what you think that matters, Valene. And I really believe that the foundation is a place where you really could make a difference. Don't let pride stand in your way."

She kissed him and smiled against his mouth. "I'll think about it."

"Okay. And when I told your mom I would like to help at the foundation, I meant it. But I promise you, I won't overstep."

"Sure you will," she teased again. "But I'm learning to lessen my resistance to your knight-in-shining-armor gig. Also, I've decided to put my condo on the market," she said softly.

He touched her cheek. "So, it looks like you will be needing somewhere to stay. Well, since you just agreed you were going to marry me, you may as well move in with me now. Besides, I need someone to pick out furniture and drapes and all that nesting kind of stuff."

"I'd love to nest here," she declared. "And marry you and have your babies. But what about the other man in my life?"

He raised a brow. "Other man?"

"Bruce," she replied. "How will he get along with Sheba? And there's no fenced yard here and I—"

"I'll build a fence," he promised. "And a huge doghouse. And a dollhouse. And a cubbyhouse for when our kids come along."

She pressed closer. "I can't wait to start our life together."

"Me either," he said.

And as he kissed her again, Jake left any doubts and insecurities behind. He was exactly where he wanted to be, with the woman of his dreams.

Life was sweet.

Epilogue

"Are you sure about this?"

Val looked up at her incredibly handsome, amazingly sexy, super-smart fiancé and nodded.

"Yes, positive. I really want to do this."

"There's no going back once we sign on the dotted line."

"I know," she said and touched his cheek. "You know, we've been talking about this all week."

"I only want you to be sure," he said and shrugged.

Val laughed softly and then sighed. It had been a whirlwind couple of weeks. First, their hasty engagement. Val had a rock on her finger that was so beautiful it defied belief. Of course, her parents had voiced their concerns about the swiftness of their relationship, but they weren't swayed. She loved Jake. He loved her. Marriage was the obvious next step. Then kids. It was everything Val had dreamed about. She had most of her personal possessions already moved into the ranch house, and other than a few furniture items left at the condo, the transition had been seamless.

She was taking a month off to get herself sorted out and then would be starting at the Fortunado Foundation. Her mother had welcomed her wholeheartedly, and even though her father was clearly disappointed she'd left the family business, he said he understood her need to do what made her happy. And both her parents adored Jake, even though they thought they were rushing into a serious relationship. Jake had gallantly asked her father for her hand, and her dad had given it—with a couple of provisos that Val wasn't privy to, as Jake had no intention of breaking her father's confidence.

But today was the big commitment day.

She got out of the truck and opened the back door, while Jake did the same on the other side. Bruce was yapping excitedly, and she grabbed his lead while Jake called a much better behaved Sheba to heel. Val was amazed at how quickly Sheba and Bruce had bonded and become good friends. Neither of them was pleased about having to use baskets to sleep in, since they had both been permanently ousted from the end of their bed. Jake had built a sturdy fence around the back of the house, and the large yard was plenty big enough for the dogs to roam around during the day. At night they spent all their time inside.

Val hadn't believed she could be so happy.

Their wedding was in the planning stage. Nothing too extravagant, although Jake had offered whatever kind of wedding she desired. But Val wasn't interested in a circus-style event. Just their families and a few close friends, with Adele and her sisters and Cassidy as attendants. She already adored Jake's younger sister and was pretty sure the feeling was reciprocated.

The wedding would take place on the ranch, down by the creek, and then a reception under a tent in Lynda's English garden. She knew it would be perfect. First, they had to get through their upcoming engagement party, which had been eagerly arranged by her family.

"Ready?"

She nodded. "Let's do it."

When they walked through the doors of the animal shelter, Florrie greeted them with wide smiles. "Hello! Everyone ready for the next big adventure?"

Val nodded, although she could see Jake was still a little skeptical. "It will work out, you'll see."

Half an hour later, they were all relieved. And delighted.

Adopting Digby had been a no-brainer. After the old dog had been passed over by the people who had put in an application a few weeks earlier, Val had secretly been delighted, because she knew he was meant to be a part of their family.

But only if he got along with Sheba and Bruce.

Which turned out just fine. Bruce bounded and slobbered around, while a more polite Sheba sniffed and then lost interest. And Digby was clearly thrilled to be put on the leash and led out to the truck. Once the three pooches were strapped in the back seat, Val jumped into the front and waited for Jake.

"All set?" he asked.

Val nodded, so happy she could barely breathe. "And raring to go."

He smiled. "I love you."

Her heart rolled over. "I love you, too."

She had so much to be grateful for. For Jake, of course, for the three happy pooches in the back, for her family, for the babies they hoped to have, for the love that had come to complete them both. And she would be eternally grateful for the silly dating app that made it all possible.

She sighed with happiness. "Let's get this adventure started."

* * * * *

Look for the next book in
The Fortunes of Texas: The Lost Fortunes
continuity, Texan Seeks Fortune
by USA TODAY *bestselling author*
Marie Ferrarella

On sale March 2019,
wherever Harlequin books
and ebooks are sold.

COMING NEXT MONTH FROM

HARLEQUIN®

SPECIAL EDITION

Available February 19, 2019

#2677 TEXAN SEEKS FORTUNE
The Fortunes of Texas: The Lost Fortunes • by Marie Ferrarella
Connor Fortunado came to Houston with only one agenda: tracking down a missing Fortune relative. His new assistant, single mom Brianna Childress, is a huge help and their attraction is instant—even though the last thing the bachelor Fortune wants is a houseful of commitments!

#2678 ANYTHING FOR HIS BABY
Crimson, Colorado • by Michelle Major
Paige Harper wants her inn, and Shep Bennett—the developer who bought it out from under her—needs a nanny. But Paige is quickly falling for little Rosie and is finding Shep more and more attractive by the day...

#2679 THE BABY ARRANGEMENT
The Daycare Chronicles • by Tara Taylor Quinn
Divorced after a heartbreaking tragedy, Mallory Harris turns to artificial insemination to have a baby. When her ex-husband learns of her plan, he offers to be the donor. Mallory needs to move on. But how can she say no to the only man she's ever loved?

#2680 THE SEAL'S SECRET DAUGHTER
American Heroes • by Christy Jeffries
When former SEAL Ethan Renault settles in Sugar Falls, Idaho, the last thing he expects to find on his doorstep...is his daughter? He's desperate for help—and librarian Monica Alvarez is just the woman for the job. But Ethan soon realizes his next mission might be to turn their no-strings romance into forever!

#2681 THE RANCHER'S RETURN
Sweet Briar Sweethearts • by Kathy Douglass
Ten years ago, the love of Raven Reynolds's life disappeared without a trace. Now Donovan Cordero is back, standing on her doorstep. Along the way, Raven had the rancher's child—though he didn't know she was pregnant! But how can she rebuild a life with her child's father if she's engaged to another man?

#2682 NOT JUST THE GIRL NEXT DOOR
Furever Yours • by Stacy Connelly
Zeke Harper has always seen Mollie McFadden as his best friend's sister. He can't cross the line, no matter how irresistible he finds the girl next door. Until Mollie makes the first move! Now Zeke wonders if this woman who opens her life to pets in need can find a place for him in her heart.

YOU CAN FIND MORE INFORMATION ON UPCOMING HARLEQUIN® TITLES, FREE EXCERPTS AND MORE AT WWW.HARLEQUIN.COM.

HSECNM0219

Get 4 FREE REWARDS!

We'll send you 2 FREE Books plus 2 FREE Mystery Gifts.

Harlequin® Special Edition books feature heroines finding the balance between their work life and personal life on the way to finding true love.

FREE Value Over **$20**

YES! Please send me 2 FREE Harlequin® Special Edition novels and my 2 FREE gifts (gifts are worth about $10 retail). After receiving them, if I don't wish to receive any more books, I can return the shipping statement marked "cancel." If I don't cancel, I will receive 6 brand-new novels every month and be billed just $4.99 per book in the U.S. or $5.74 per book in Canada. That's a savings of at least 12% off the cover price! It's quite a bargain! Shipping and handling is just 50¢ per book in the U.S. and 75¢ per book in Canada.* I understand that accepting the 2 free books and gifts places me under no obligation to buy anything. I can always return a shipment and cancel at any time. The free books and gifts are mine to keep no matter what I decide.

235/335 HDN GMY2

Name (please print)

Address   Apt. #

City   State/Province   Zip/Postal Code

Mail to the **Reader Service:**
IN U.S.A.: P.O. Box 1341, Buffalo, NY 14240-8531
IN CANADA: P.O. Box 603, Fort Erie, Ontario L2A 5X3

Want to try 2 free books from another series? Call 1-800-873-8635 or visit www.ReaderService.com.

---

*Terms and prices subject to change without notice. Prices do not include sales taxes, which will be charged (if applicable) based on your state or country of residence. Canadian residents will be charged applicable taxes. Offer not valid in Quebec. This offer is limited to one order per household. Books received may not be as shown. Not valid for current subscribers to Harlequin® Special Edition books. All orders subject to approval. Credit or debit balances in a customer's account(s) may be offset by any other outstanding balance owed by or to the customer. Please allow 4 to 6 weeks for delivery. Offer available while quantities last.

Your Privacy—The Reader Service is committed to protecting your privacy. Our Privacy Policy is available online at www.ReaderService.com or upon request from the Reader Service. We make a portion of our mailing list available to reputable third parties that offer products we believe may interest you. If you prefer that we not exchange your name with third parties, or if you wish to clarify or modify your communication preferences, please visit us at www.ReaderService.com/consumerschoice or write to us at Reader Service Preference Service, P.O. Box 9062, Buffalo, NY 14240-9062. Include your complete name and address.

HSE19R

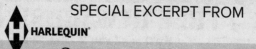
"You'll still get plenty of time with him," Raven said as Elias
ran off.

"You're being nicer about this than I'd expected you to be."

"What did you think I'd do? Grab my kid and go sneaking off
in the middle of the night?"

Donovan inhaled a sharp breath.

"Sorry. I didn't mean that the way it sounded."

"I'm just a bit sensitive, I guess."

"And I'm a bit uncomfortable. Have you noticed how many
people are staring at us?"

"They're not staring at us. They're staring at you. You're the
prettiest girl here."

Raven laughed. "There's no need for flattery. I already said you
can spend time with Elias."

"It's not flattery. It's the truth. You're gorgeous."

The laughter vanished from her voice and the sparkle left her eyes. "No flirting. We're not on a date. We're here for Elias."

"But we are getting to know each other. Not for the purpose of falling in love again. I know you're engaged and I respect that."

"Who told you I was engaged?"

"Carson. Congratulations, I hope you'll be happy together. Just so you know, I have no intention of interfering in your life. But if we're going to coparent Elias, we need to find a way to be friends again. And we were friends, weren't we?"

She nodded and the smile reappeared. Apparently he'd said the right thing.

Donovan stepped in front of Raven and took her hands in his. Though she worked on the ranch, her palms were soft. "I'm sorry."

"Sorry for what?"

"For putting you through ten years of hell. Ten years of hoping I'd come home. For not being around while you were pregnant or to help you raise our son. All of it. I'm sorry for all of it. Please forgive me."

Her eyes widened in surprise and she blinked. Was what he'd said so unexpected? He didn't think so. Just what kind of jerk did she think he'd become? He replayed the conversation they'd had that first night. It must have looked like he was playing games when he hadn't fully answered her questions. But Raven was engaged to another man, so his reasons for staying away really didn't matter now. They'd have to start here to build their relationship.

"You're forgiven."

"Clean slate?"

She smiled. "Clean slate. Now let's catch up to Elias and play some games. I plan on winning one of those oversize teddy bears."

Don't miss
The Rancher's Return *by Kathy Douglass,*
available March 2019 wherever
Harlequin® Special Edition books and ebooks are sold.

www.Harlequin.com

#1 *New York Times* bestselling author

LINDA LAEL MILLER

presents:

The next great contemporary read from
Harlequin Special Edition author Kathy Douglass!
A heartwarming story about finding community,
friendship and even love.

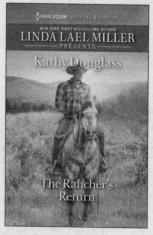

"That's all you have to
say? You're back now?"

Ten years ago, the love
of Raven Reynolds's life
disappeared without a trace.
Now Donovan Cordero
is back, standing on her
doorstep. Along the way,
Raven had the rancher's
child—though he didn't
know she was pregnant!
Now her prayers have been
answered, but happily-ever-
after feels further away than
ever. Because how can she rebuild a life with her child's
father if she's engaged to another man?

**Available February 19,
wherever books are sold.**

www.Harlequin.com

HSELLM57364